So here she was in league with the sheriff. It was a strange bonding, one fraught with frightening possibilities. At any moment he could decide the risk of harboring her was too great.

Josh sat down on the bed beside her and wrapped his arm around her trembling shoulders. She rested against him, as soft as a pillow of clover. And then his lips were on hers, and even vestiges of sane thought were stripped from his mind.

He knew he was making a monumental mistake. But still he didn't pull away.

Chrysie trembled as Josh's lips claimed hers. The passion surging through her was almost as frightening as the fear, the sweet, salty taste of Josh's mouth foreign and forbidden. It was the wrong time, the wrong place, the wrong man. But the kiss deepened, and she couldn't fight the thrill of Josh McCain along with everything else she had to battle.

MAVERICK
CHRISTMAS

JOANNA WAYNE

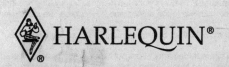

TORONTO • NEW YORK • LONDON
AMSTERDAM • PARIS • SYDNEY • HAMBURG
STOCKHOLM • ATHENS • TOKYO • MILAN • MADRID
PRAGUE • WARSAW • BUDAPEST • AUCKLAND

A heartfelt thanks to Paula Haines, Jay Miller, Vicki Sucher and Joyce Keiler, my golfing buddies who keep me sane. And always, a special word of appreciation to my wonderful editor Denise Zaza, who puts up with me. A hug to my husband, who has the patience to live with a writer. And most especially, happy holidays to all my fantastic and very loyal readers.

ISBN-13: 978-0-373-22955-0
ISBN-10: 0-373-22955-0

MAVERICK CHRISTMAS

Copyright © 2006 by Jo Ann Vest

www.eHarlequin.com

Printed in U.S.A.

ABOUT THE AUTHOR

Joanna Wayne lives with her husband just a few miles from steamy, exciting New Orleans, but her home is the perfect writer's hideaway. A lazy bayou, complete with graceful herons, colorful wood ducks and an occasional alligator, winds just below her back garden. When not creating tales of spine-tingling suspense and heartwarming romance, she enjoys reading, traveling, playing golf and spending time with family and friends.

Joanna believes that one of the special joys of writing is knowing that her stories have brought enjoyment to or somehow touched the lives of her readers. You can write Joanna at P.O. Box 2851, Harvey, LA 70059-2851.

Books by Joanna Wayne

CAST OF CHARACTERS

Chrysie Atwater—Child psychologist on the run who thinks Montana will be her haven, until she crosses paths with the handsome sheriff.

Sheriff Josh McCain—He'll break every rule in the book to keep Chrysie and her daughters safe.

Jenny and Mandy—Chrysie's two preschool daughters.

Danny and Davy McCain—The sheriff's six-year-old twin sons.

Logan and Rachel McCain—Josh's brother and sister-in-law.

Jonathan Harwell—Chrysie's murdered husband, a man with lots of secrets.

Buck and Evelyn Miller—The cabin that Chrysie rents in Montana is on their land.

Cougar—The part-time deputy.

Vanessa Templar—Ex-secretary and possible lover of Chrysie's late husband.

Luisa Pellot—Jonathan Harwell's law partner before he was killed.

Angela Martina and Juan Hernandez—Houston homicide detectives.

Mac Buckley and Sean Rogers—Paid killers.

Grecco—Josh's friend, who works for Homeland Security.

Chapter One

Chrysie Atwater rushed across the creaking floor of the civic center to pick up her young angel, who'd just been shoved to the floor by the unruly reindeer. The boy and his twin brother had been out of control all night, totally undisciplined and requiring constant supervision.

"I want to go home," Jenny announced as Chrysie helped her back to her feet and straightened her wings.

"You don't want to let one reindeer keep you from being in the pageant."

"He's not a reindeer. He's just an annoying boy."

A very astute judgment, but Chrysie wasn't ready to pull Jenny out of the performance. Both of her young daughters needed some normalcy and social interaction with their peers, especially Jenny. Moving from town to town had been stressful for her.

Which was why Chrysie was out on a frigid night,

volunteering her services to Jenny's kindergarten teacher, who'd taken on the unenviable task of directing the community Christmas pageant.

Mrs. Larkey had the reindeer collared and was leading him toward them. "Tell Jenny you're sorry, Danny," she said.

"I'm sorry," he said, stamping at the floor like a frisky pony and showing no sign of remorse. In fact, mischief danced in his dark eyes.

"No more pushing," Mrs. Larkey said. "If you do, I'll have to tell your father."

"Aw, don't tell him. I'll be good." The kid looked up at the teacher and smiled, showing a gap in front where one of his baby teeth was missing.

Chrysie followed Mrs. Larkey as she walked back to the stage to corral the singing Christmas trees, who were rummaging through the toys that were meant to be props. "Are those two boys always so disruptive?" she asked.

"Pretty much," Mrs. Larkey said. "Such a shame when their father is so nice."

"It's none of my business, but…" She let the comment drop. *None of her business* was the operative phrase here.

"Okay, Christmas trees," Mrs. Larkey said, "put down the toys and get back on the platform. You have to be ready to sing as soon as Santa Claus delivers the bad news to the reindeer."

She turned back to Chrysie. "The sheriff does the best he can, but the boys are just too much for him."

The Sheriff. Chrysie groaned inwardly. If she'd known the sheriff or any other lawman was even remotely connected to the pageant, she'd never have volunteered or let the girls participate. Better if the guy didn't even know she existed.

She turned away just in time to see Danny's brother crash into the Christmas tree they were using as the main prop. The tree rocked back and forth a second, then toppled to the floor, eliciting piercing squeals from the young girls who'd been standing under it and loud laughs from the boys.

Instinctively Chrysie grabbed the guilty child by the arm. "That was not funny, young man. You could have hurt someone."

"Leggo of me. It was an accident."

"An accident that wouldn't have happened if you'd been practicing with the other reindeer."

"Daddy!" The deafening holler played havoc on her eardrums.

The boy broke away from her and rushed down the steps, hurling himself into the arms of a cowboy who'd apparently come in the back door unnoticed.

A gorgeous, dark-haired hunk of a cowboy. Wouldn't you know?

"Is there a problem?"

"Your son knocked over the Christmas tree."

"It was an accident, Daddy."

The cowboy walked up on the stage, looking tough and incredibly sexy. He rocked back on his heels and studied the tree. "Tree looks like it survived. Was anyone hurt?"

"Everyone's fine, Sheriff McCain." He'd directed the question at Chrysie, but Mrs. Larkey had rushed over and answered for her.

"Then I guess no harm was done." The sheriff picked up the tree and set it in an upright position. "How's that?" he said, standing back to see if the tree was straight.

Mrs. Larkey smiled up at him as if he'd accomplished some miraculous act. "It looks perfect, Sheriff McCain."

The woman was married, and the guy still had her eating out of his hands. Chrysie stepped between Mrs. Larkey and the sheriff. "Actually, it's not quite perfect. It's leaning toward the left."

Mrs. Larkey looked from the tree to Chrysie, then shook her head as if she thought Chrysie was wrong. But she gathered the children and sent them back to their places.

The sheriff ignored the tree and looked Chrysie right in the eye. "Everything looks fine to me."

"The tree is leaning."

"If you say so." He adjusted the angle. "Does that

suit you? If not, I can always move it another fiftieth of an inch."

"Now it's leaning to the right."

He eyed it critically. "Looks straight to me, but maybe I'm just not quite as uptight about Christmas trees as you."

"It was straight before—" She caught herself before she said more. It was the stress of the situation that was getting to her, stress that had nothing to do with Christmas or the sheriff's son. "Tree's fine," she said, then turned her back on him and walked away.

She could kick herself for having said anything at all to the man. Riling the sheriff was the last thing she needed. Keeping a low profile was the name of the game—and the game was staying alive.

"EAT YOUR CEREAL, Danny."

"I am eating."

"Eat faster. It's snowing, and driving will be a…" Josh McCain bit back the word he would have used before the boys had come to live with him. Who'd have thought two small boys could turn his life totally upside down?

"Daddy, Davy's slurping his hot chocolate, and my teacher said it's bad manners to slurp."

"That's just when you're at school, right, Daddy? Cowboys can slurp at home."

"Best not to." Josh grabbed a piece of cold toast

as he passed the table. He only managed to wolf down one bite before his cell phone jangled.

"Sheriff McCain."

"Sheriff, this is Cindy Gathers. I really hate to call you with this, but you're going to have to find someone else to keep the boys after school. I thought I could handle it, but it's just too much on me what with my arthritis and all."

He groaned. It was the fourth sitter he'd lost in six months. The boys went through them almost as fast as they went through a box of cereal.

"I hope you can give me time to find another sitter before you bail on me."

"I'm sorry about this, Sheriff, real sorry, but I just don't think I can handle them another day. You know how it is. I love them, but they just don't mind. It's worse than riding herd over wild horses."

"They're just being boys."

Danny jumped down from the table and went tearing down the hall with Davy hot on his trail.

"You hit me first."

"Did not."

"Did so."

A little undisciplined, Josh admitted to himself, but they weren't bad kids. The problem was probably more his fault than theirs.

He didn't know squat about raising kids. Cattle, yeah. That he could handle. Even sheriffing seemed to come naturally to him. But fatherhood had him over a barrel. It had just come at him too fast and with too little warning.

His cell phone rang again. This time it was Bonehead up on Highway 12. Someone had cut some of his fences, and a couple of his prize bulls had gotten out. He figured it was the Grayson boys since he'd demanded they pay for a sheep they'd shot when they were hunting on his land. Josh promised he'd be out to check the fences as soon as he dropped the boys off to school.

"I'm counting to five," Josh yelled. "You best be in the truck and ready to go to school by the time I finish." Normally they would have ridden the school bus, but he'd let them sleep a little later since he had to make a trip into town this morning anyway.

It took three more warnings to get the boys and their book bags into the backseat of his double-cab pickup truck. The snow was falling pretty good, but the weatherman hadn't predicted anything but flurries today. The real storm wasn't due until tomorrow.

They were almost to school when he spotted the blue compact car parked at the side of the road with the hood up. He pulled up behind the vehicle. The woman who'd been staring at the engine waved and smiled. He didn't recognize her until the hood of her parka blew off and he caught sight of her short blond hair snaring snowflakes.

It was the woman who'd gotten all bent out of shape last night over the Christmas tree mishap at the civic center. Obviously she wasn't as demanding that her husband keep her car in good working order. But then, if you had a woman that cute around the house, you might have better things to do than work on cars.

"The motor died on me," she said as he walked up. "And then it wouldn't start again."

He looked around under the hood, but didn't see anything obvious. "Probably the battery," he said. "I can give you a jump."

"I'd appreciate that."

"I'll get the cables and be right back. You can wait in the car if you like."

"I'd definitely like. Are winters always this cold in Montana?"

"It'll get a lot colder than this. Where are you from?"

"The South."

"That covers a wide area. I'd guess Texas, judging from your accent." If he was right, she didn't admit it. "What brings you to Montana?"

"Just wanted a change of scenery."

"Are you and your husband ranchers?"

"No."

He strode to the truck, checked on the boys—who were arguing about whether *Ice Age* or *Ice Age 2* was the better movie—then returned with the jumper cables. It didn't take but a minute to bring the engine to life.

The woman put her head out the car window. "I really appreciate the help, Sheriff."

"No problem."

"Can I pay you?"

"A good cowboy doesn't take pay for helping a lady in distress."

He clapped his hands together to warm them. "Your husband needs to replace that battery. It's going to be a long winter, and you don't want to risk getting stuck out in a blizzard."

"Thanks. I'll see that it's done. Are you sure I can't pay you for your trouble?"

Actually, he did need a favor. But she had two little girls sitting in the car with her right now. What would she know about caring for two rambunctious first-grade boys? For that matter, what did he know about it?

"I don't think we've officially met," he said, lingering by her car while he figured out if he dared leave his boys with this woman—even if she agreed to watch them. "I'm Josh McCain. I'm the local sheriff."

"I'm Chrysie Atwater." She ran her hands over the steering wheel, clearly ready to be off. Her children were sitting in the car, talking to each other in nice, quiet voices. He could hear his boys from where he was standing. She must know something about tending kids.

"If you really want to thank me, you could do me a favor."

"What would that be?"

"I'm kind of in a bind. I have an important meeting with the county prosecutor this afternoon, and my sitter can't watch the boys. I'd be much obliged if you'd watch them for me for a couple of hours."

"Just for today?"

"That's all I'm asking."

"I suppose I could do that."

"I'll pay you the going rate."

"No, that's not necessary," she said. "I'll be repaying your favor."

"Where do you live?"

"We're renting the foreman's cabin on Buck Miller's ranch."

"So your husband works for Buck?"

"No. I'll take the boys home with me after school if you'd like. You can pick them up at my house when you've finished your meeting."

"Sounds like a deal."

She nodded and dropped her gear into Drive. The second he stepped away from the car, she revved the engine and pulled back onto the highway.

There was something about her that bothered him. He couldn't quite put his finger on it, but something all the same. He figured her for a socialite, a woman used to getting her way. He'd been around enough of those in his younger days to recognize them a mile away.

Not that she was a snob. *Refined* was probably the

better word. And she didn't seem that fond of cold weather for a lady who'd just moved from the South to Montana for a change in scenery.

He'd give Buck's wife a call and he'd stop and see Mrs. Larkey, as well. Unless they gave her a glowing recommendation, he'd just have to cancel the meeting with the D.A. The meeting was important, but the boys came first. He might not be the best of fathers, but he loved them like crazy. That had to count for something.

CHRYSIE WAS DOWN on her hands and knees scrubbing the old wooden floors with a vengeance when she heard the knock at the door. Apprehension hit as always, sending her pulse racing and her insides rolling. She jumped to her feet and ran to the window, not breathing easy until she spotted Evelyn Miller at the door.

She peeled the yellow rubber gloves from her hands and dropped them near the bucket of soapy water. It took several seconds to unlatch the triple security locks she'd installed herself and open the door.

"I was making us a rhubarb pie for dessert," Evelyn said, smiling broadly. "So I made one for you and the girls, too."

"That was thoughtful."

"No more trouble to make two than one." Evelyn handed her the pie. "You sure have this place sparkling. It hasn't been this clean since Buck and the hands built it some thirty years ago."

"I've enjoyed working on it." Strangely that was the truth. Other than run the vacuum cleaner, she'd never done any heavy housework. But this was the closest thing she'd had to a real house since she'd lived in Houston. And that was only because the Millers had rented it to her for less than she'd paid for that crummy apartment they'd lived in before settling in Montana.

Evelyn straightened the stained apron that puckered around her plump waist and broad hips. She was short, probably no more than a couple of inches over five feet, big-boned, with more than ample breasts that drooped nearly to her waist and short brown hair that frizzed about her reddened cheeks. But her genuine smile and dancing eyes radiated warmth.

"I'd ask you to sit down and visit a while," Chrysie said, "but I need to get this scrubbing finished before I have to pick up the girls." Chrysie made sure she was always early to pick them up, Mandy first from the preschool class at the Methodist church next door to the school, then Jenny from kindergarten.

"You go right ahead. I'll just visit with you while you work."

Not exactly what Chrysie wanted to hear, but there wasn't a lot she could do about it. Not that Evelyn wasn't nice or that Chrysie couldn't use a little adult female company, but making friends always led to questions. And questions led to lies.

"Most of the ranchers don't bother with preschool for their kids. It's just too much hassle driving into town every day."

"Mandy only goes three days a week, and I like for her to have some social interaction with peers." But this was the first time she'd ever enrolled either of them in anything that kept them out of her sight for any stretch of time. She was still very uneasy with it.

"You must have met the sheriff on one of your trips into town."

Chrysie's breath caught, and she turned away so Evelyn wouldn't see that the comment had caught her off guard. "How do you know that?"

"He called this morning asking about you. I think he might have taken a liking to you. You're the best-looking woman around here, and that's for sure."

"What did he ask?"

"He just wanted to know what I thought of you."

"What did you tell him?"

"That you were a real nice lady and a great mom."

"Was that it?"

"Pretty much. But I think he might come a-calling."

"He's only interested in my qualifications as a babysitter. I've offered to fill in for his regular sitter this afternoon."

Chrysie put on the gloves again and dropped to her knees. She'd have to work fast to finish this before she had to shower and leave for town. Buying the new battery had eaten up most of the morning and a chunk of her remaining cash.

She could probably make it through the winter on what she'd saved if they didn't have too many emergencies, but she'd have to find at least part-time work by spring. Spring in Montana would be nice, but she never counted on being anywhere that long.

Evelyn sashayed around the edges of the damp floor. "The sheriff is a bachelor, you know. And those kids of his sure need a mother."

"What happened to theirs?"

"No one really knows. He left here last year and came back with two sons and a new last name. He didn't do a lot of explaining."

"And no one asked?"

"No. That's the way it is up here. A man's business is his own."

Hopefully that worked for women, as well.

"Sheriff asked about your husband. I told him you were a widow. That is what you said, isn't it? That your husband was dead?"

Chrysie nodded. That was the one thing she hadn't lied about.

"I should get Buck to paint this place for you. The hands aren't all that busy in the winter. He could probably spare a couple of them for a day or two."

"That would be great." Chrysie looked up from the floor and stared at the dingy walls. "A yellow would really brighten up the house, maybe the color of daffodils."

"Walls like a spring daffodil?" Evelyn looked around as if seeing the house for the first time. "I was thinking white, but yellow might be nice. Come to think of it, my kitchen could use some brightening, too."

Evelyn stayed a few more minutes, then walked over to the door to let herself out. "You sure have yourself locked in here."

"I like to feel safe, especially for the girls."

"There's no trouble here on the ranch. Buck wouldn't have it. Someone come messing around here, he'd shoot them full of lead. Nobody messes with anything on Buck's property."

"That's good to know." But the locks would stay.

"Give some thought to what I said about the sheriff, Chrysie. He's a good man. Nice-looking, too. All the young, single women in town are after him all the time—not that there are that many young, single women around."

"I'll give it some thought."

After Evelyn left, Chrysie finished the floor, then dumped the dirty water outside. She stood for a minute, letting the frigid air fill her lungs while she took in the magnificent mountain view.

This place was so perfect. Clean air. A decent house for practically no rent. A small, friendly community that had accepted them with a minimum of questions. She just had to make sure it stayed that way.

Which meant she needed Sheriff Josh McCain to forget she existed.

A good catch, maybe. But not for a fugitive from justice.

Chapter Two

The snow had been no more than occasional flurries for most of the day, but it began to fall harder just as Josh turned onto the road to Buck Miller's house. Before he'd come to Montana, he'd thought of snow only in terms of powder quality for skiing. Now it was a way of life.

The frigid temperatures had been a rough adjustment to a Louisiana man's system that first winter. Physical labor had been a new experience, as well. But poverty had been the real shocker. He'd never realized how important money was until he didn't have any.

Buck had given him his first real job. The old rancher and the rest of the hands figured out pretty quickly what a greenhorn Josh was. He got all the dirty work that first year, had gone to bed with aching muscles and new calluses on top of old. But the work had accomplished what years of spending his father's money and playing with the druggies on the streets of the Big Easy couldn't—it had made him a man.

No one had asked Josh why he'd moved to Montana. They judged him by the job he did and his willingness to help out where needed. It was the way of life up here and the reason Josh had stayed.

He should give Chrysie Atwater the benefit of that same philosophy, but he was having trouble doing that, especially after talking to Evelyn and Mrs. Larkey about her.

He never underestimated a woman's ability to do most things a man could do. Some of the biggest spreads in the state were owned and run by women. But Chrysie wasn't Montana-bred. She was a single mother from the South who'd moved to a small town pretty much in the middle of nowhere where she had no job, no friends and no family. It just didn't add up, and things that didn't add up always made Josh suspicious.

But unlike everyone else who'd tried lately, she seemed quite capable of managing his sons. He'd checked on them several times this afternoon, and their complaints had assured him they were being well cared for.

Danny had said Mrs. Atwater was bossy and made him practice his reading. And Davy had whined that she made him wear his snow pants when he went outside to play and gave him fruit for his afternoon snack instead of the candy and soda he'd wanted.

Even more impressive, Chrysie had sounded calm on the telephone when he'd asked her about the boys. That in itself put her in a whole new class as far as his experience with sitters was concerned.

Not that the sexy Mrs. Atwater was perfect. Last night's tree-falling incident had proved that the woman was wound a tad too tightly for Josh's liking. But what the hell. Josh was desperate for someone to watch the boys on a daily basis, and she might be the ideal solution.

That is, if she checked out. Before he could ascertain that, he'd need to find out exactly what had brought her to Aohkii, Montana.

THE AFTERNOON HAD been every bit as stressful as Chrysie had expected. The boys were incorrigible, constantly pushing the limits. It was clear they'd never been disciplined appropriately. She'd love to point out to Josh McCain all the ways he was failing his sons, but she didn't dare. The less interaction she had with the sheriff, the better.

She glanced at the clock above the kitchen counter. Six-thirty, and he wasn't back yet. For the minute, both Davy and Danny were under control, wolfing down sloppy joes as though they hadn't eaten in weeks. Jenny and Mandy were taking their usual small bites and dawdling between each mouthful.

"Can I have more?" Danny asked.

"You surely can."

"Me, too," Davy said, shoving the rest of his food into his mouth. "Daddy's sloppy joes aren't this good."

"Sloppy joes, floppy joes, up your nose," Danny said as she refilled his plate.

Mandy giggled as if he'd said something remarkably witty. Jenny ignored him. At five, she was not nearly as impressed with the boys' antics as her three-year-old sister.

"Davy kicked me under the table," Jenny complained.

"Did not."

"Did so."

"I was just swinging my foot and your leg got in the way."

"Stop swinging your foot at the table," Chrysie ordered.

"My dad lets me."

"I'm not your dad," she said, glancing out the window as she heard an approaching vehicle. She all but shouted her relief when she saw it was the sheriff's black pickup truck.

A minute later Chrysie opened the back door, and both boys jumped from their chairs as if shot from cannons and raced to smother their father in hugs. She wasn't sure if that was their usual greeting or if they were just thrilled to be rescued from her.

The sheriff removed his black Stetson and raked

his fingers through his thick, dark hair, smoothing the strands the hat had mussed. "Something smells good."

"Yeah, Mrs. Atwater made sloppy joes. And they're really good. She doesn't put those yucky onions in them like you do, Daddy."

"Guess I'll have to get her recipe."

Davy climbed back in his chair. "Can my daddy have some, too?"

"If he'd like. There's plenty," Chrysie said. She didn't consider that much of an invitation, but apparently it was all the sheriff needed. He shrugged out of his parka and hung it on one of the coat hooks near the door.

He was not the kind of man a woman could just ignore, she admitted as she felt his dark, piercing gaze follow her as she grabbed an extra plate from the cupboard.

He took the only available spot—the chair at the end of the table opposite hers. She filled the plate and set it in front of him. "You can have water, milk or coffee," she said. "I'm afraid that's all I can offer."

"Milk sounds good."

She poured him a glass, then joined them at the table, though her appetite had vanished. Apprehension did that to her, and there was no way she could not be anxious as long as a man with a badge was in her house.

Jenny ran the fork around her plate, using the

prongs to make a design in the sauce, before looking at Chrysie with pleading eyes.

"May I be excused?"

Chrysie stared at her daughter's half-full plate. "You didn't eat much."

"I'm full."

"Me, too," Mandy said.

"Okay, you can take your plates to the sink. But it's a long time until breakfast."

Both girls wiped their faces and hands on their napkins, then cleared their dishes from the table. With them gone, the boys clamored all the louder for Josh's attention, both talking at once, trying to top each other's stories. They thrived on his attention, devouring it the way they'd gulped down their food.

That need for approval and affirmation could well be at the root of much of their truculent behavior, especially if they'd been neglected or had experienced a major emotional trauma in their past.

"Sounds as if you guys had a busy afternoon," Josh said.

"Yeah, but we didn't have any fun," Danny complained. "Too many rules."

"Yeah, too many rules," Davy agreed, mimicking as always.

Danny cleaned his plate for the second time, then jumped down from his chair and started back to the living room, where the girls were. Davy followed him.

"Whoa!" Josh said. "You heard Mrs. Atwater. Take your plates to the sink. Rules of the house."

Danny turned and stared at his dad as if he'd asked him to grow wings. "We don't have to do that at home."

"We might just start it."

The boys muttered under their breaths but surprisingly complied without more argument. Once the plates were deposited, Danny shoved Davy and ran from the kitchen. Davy took off after him for payback.

Josh shook his head. "Guess I need to work on their manners."

"Wouldn't hurt," Chrysie agreed.

"I really appreciate your helping out with them. I could have canceled the meeting today if it came to that, but the D.A. wouldn't have been too happy about it. He really wants to nail old Jake Mahoney."

She nodded but didn't respond, hoping that would put an end to the conversation.

Josh cleaned his plate, then gulped down the rest of his milk. Apparently the boys got their appetite from him.

"I guess you probably heard about Jake," Josh said.

"No."

"He's pretty much the talk of the town these days. He seemed nice enough until he came unglued and shot and killed a couple of the hands working with him."

"He must have had some provocation."

"Claimed the guys were horsing around and not

pulling their share of the load. Shocked everyone who knew him until we found out Jake had been committed to a mental hospital down in Mississippi a few years back for attacking his father with a knife. Don't know what those shrinks were thinking letting him out."

"You can't blame the psychiatrists or psychologists for this."

"Yeah? Who would you blame?"

"There can be any number of factors…." She stopped midsentence—before she said too much.

"Sorry," Josh said. "I guess murders aren't the best topic for dinner conversation. Fortunately we don't have many around here. If we did, that wouldn't leave me a lot of time for running the Double D."

"Is that your ranch?"

"Yeah. I changed the name of it after I took custody of Danny and Davy. Before that it was called Timber Trails. Don't know where that name came from. I bought the land from some actor out in California who'd bought the ranch but never lived on it."

"I guess ranching isn't everyone's cup of tea."

"Probably no one's cup of tea. This is more a strong-coffee or cold-beer world. People either love it or hate it. So what brings you out here, Chrysie? You don't seem like a woman with ranching in your blood."

So it was Chrysie now. This morning it had been Mrs. Atwater. She liked it better when he used her last name. This way it seemed they were friends, and she definitely didn't want him to get that idea.

"I don't plan on ranching."

"So what are you planning to do?"

"Raise my daughters."

"Do their grandparents live in—where was it you said you were from? Texas?"

"No." Chrysie gathered the rest of the dishes from the table and carried them to the counter, then started to fill the sink with soapy water. Surely he'd take the hint and leave.

He didn't. Or else he ignored it. He followed her to the sink. "You wash and I'll dry."

"That's not necessary."

"It's the least I can do after you watched the boys for me all afternoon."

She dipped her hands into the bubbles. "I was returning a favor. Now we're even."

"I doubt that. The boys are a lot more work than a battery jump."

Josh grabbed the dish towel from the counter and took a freshly rinsed plate from her hand. The seemingly meaningless exchange shot her apprehension level straight up.

"I know they're not the best-behaved kids in the world," Josh continued. "I try, but I hate to be too hard on them. And I'm not a natural at the discipline thing, like you seem to be. I figured if I didn't get that tree straight enough to suit you, you'd take me out behind the woodshed for a switching."

"I don't spank."

"Well, there goes that fantasy."

Her cheeks burned at his teasing, and she got so rattled she almost let the plate she was washing slip from her fingers. She gritted her teeth, furious with herself that she could show any weakness with a man who held so much potential for disaster. She glued her gaze to the sink and the few remaining dishes.

Josh dried the last fork, then scanned the kitchen. "This house is nice."

"It's quite comfortable," she agreed.

"Twice the size of mine. I'm planning to build a bigger place when I get the time, but I've been concentrating on getting the ranch fixed up first." He slapped his right hand on the tile counter. "I like this tile, too. I know Buck's current foreman has his own place, a small ranch about twenty miles north of here, but I hadn't heard Buck was renting out his cabin. How did you find out about it?"

"I asked around town, and someone at Humphries Bar and Grill mentioned it was empty and that the Millers might be willing to rent it."

"How did you ever land in Aohkii to start with?"

"I read about the town in a travel magazine," she said, sticking to the story she'd concocted on her first day here. "I was looking for an inexpensive place to settle where there were four seasons and a safe environment for my girls, and this seemed like it."

"A travel magazine, huh? Which one?"

"I don't remember."

"Too bad. I'm sure the locals would love to read that article."

It was clear from his tone and the way he was looking at her that he didn't buy her story. "Where did the twins live before you took custody?" she asked, determined to move the focus of the conversation away from her.

"New Orleans."

"That's a long way from Montana."

"Another world. Have you ever been there?"

"I went to Mardi Gras once when—" She stopped. Every time she opened her mouth, she gave something away. "When I was in my early twenties, before the girls were born."

"They're cute girls."

"They're my life."

"I can tell." He turned his gaze to the rhubarb pie. "You're a pretty amazing woman to manage Danny and Davy and still find time to bake."

"Evelyn Miller made the pie."

"It looks great. Bet it would be good with a cup of coffee about now."

Sure. Her and the sheriff having coffee and pie in the cozy kitchen while their children played together in the living room and a quiet snow fell just outside the frosted windows.

"No coffee for me," she said. "But you're more than welcome to half the pie. I'll cut it and wrap it in foil while you get the boys into their coats and boots." She could not possibly make it any plainer that it was time for him to leave.

Instead of walking away, Josh stepped closer. "Is everything okay?"

Her insides shook. "Why wouldn't it be?"

"I don't know. I just get the impression that something's bothering you."

Dread swelled until she could barely breathe. She had to play this cooler, seem more like a woman with nothing to hide. She should have invited him to stay for pie and coffee, but then that might have led to even more mistakes.

"I'm fine, Sheriff, just tired."

She found herself holding her breath until he'd turned and left the room. She made him a pie doggie bag, then went to tell the boys goodbye.

"Are we coming back here tomorrow?" Davy asked.

"Not tomorrow," Josh said.

"Then who's going to watch us?" Danny asked.

The concern in his young voice got to Chrysie, but there was too much at stake here for her to consider anyone except Jenny and Mandy.

"Don't worry," Josh assured his sons, "I'll make

certain you're in good hands. Now go hop in the truck and buckle up."

Chrysie stepped to the door and breathed in a huge gulp of the cold air as the boys raced to the truck. Unfortunately Josh didn't race away with them.

"If you need anything, Chrysie, anything at all, just give me a call."

She swallowed hard and shivered, chilled by the cold wind and the realization of how badly she wished she could open up to someone. But she couldn't. She couldn't rely on anyone but herself.

Even now, she'd have to start thinking about moving on. Aohkii was no more the refuge she'd hoped for than any of her other stops had been. Safety for her and her daughters was never more than an illusion.

CHRYSIE ATWATER HAD managed to do what few women in Josh McCain's life ever had. She'd kept him awake and thinking about her most of the night. But it wasn't Chrysie's good looks and great body that had caused the insomnia. Not the way her short blond hair curled around her cheeks, either. It wasn't even about the way her jeans rode her hips, low and tight so that the back pockets seemed to be cradling her cute little butt.

It was none of that, he assured himself. It was only that she was the first person in a long time who'd handled his sons for an entire afternoon without seeming ready for the loony bin. More important, in spite of the boys' complaints about her last night, over breakfast this morning they'd both asked if they could go back to her house after school. She hadn't offered her services, of course, but that didn't worry him. His powers of persuasion with the opposite sex were legend.

But so were his instinctive hunches, and Chrysie's behavior last night had raised a couple of bright red flags. She'd been far too quick to change the subject when he'd tried to ask her about herself.

And then there was that story of reading about Aohkii in a travel magazine. Aohkii was so little it wasn't even on most maps. The town's only claim to fame was Ted Greely's collection of rodeo buckles, and he hadn't ridden a bronc since he'd been thrown and kicked in the head down in Wyoming.

Josh dropped to the worn leather chair in his office, punched a few keys on his computer and brought up the Web site for the national law enforcers' listing of missing persons. No use to type in Chrysie Atwater. People on the run never used their own name.

He considered possibilities as the Web site continued to load. He couldn't see Chrysie as a hardened criminal, but she might have taken her daughters and escaped an abusive husband. Women did that all the time, though frankly Chrysie didn't seem the type to run from anything.

But then, this might be a case of kidnapping by the noncustodial parent. He could see her taking matters into her own hands if a judge had given her husband custody of the girls. But why move here? And what was she using for money?

Josh typed in the parameters for the search. Within the last three years, since he was pretty sure Mandy was no older than that. A mother and her two children, approximate ages between two and six years. That should do for starters.

He hit the search key and waited. The list that came up seemed endless. He added a new criterion: disappeared from Texas.

The modified list was still long but more manageable. He skimmed quickly, hoping for a recognizable image of one of the three. None of the pictures triggered any kind of recognition—not until he was almost through the list. Even then, the actual picture didn't show a lot of similarity to the girls, but the computer-generated likeness to predict what the older girl might look like today showed a distinct resemblance to Jenny Atwater.

Last seen with their mother, Dr. Cassandra Harwell. Josh studied the grainy photo of the woman. Her hair was dark and cut in a short bob. She was wearing a plain business suit with a tailored blouse. She was paler and much thinner than Chrysie, almost gaunt.

Yet there was something about the photo that

reminded him of Chrysie. Maybe the eyes. And the mouth, upturned slightly as if she were forcing a smile. Chrysie had smiled that same way last night.

Reluctantly Josh hit the accompanying hot key for more information.

Sara Elizabeth and Rebecca Marie Harwell, disappeared November 6, 2003, from Houston, Texas. Believed to be in the company of their mother, Dr. Cassandra Blankenship Harwell, a child psychologist in Houston.

Dr. Harwell was wanted for questioning in the shooting death of her husband Jonathan Harwell and was considered a prime suspect in his murder.

Chapter Three

The information sent a couple of shock waves to Josh's brain. He'd heard of man killers who looked like innocent babes before, but he'd never expected to run into one at the local civic center. But if it turned out Chrysie and the missing doctor from Texas were one and the same, he'd not only run into her but had left Danny and Davy in her care.

The heat in his office kicked on, and Josh shrugged out of his jacket as he skimmed the sparse facts. Jonathan Hawthorne Harwell, a Houston attorney, had been found murdered in his bed. His wife and their two children had gone missing four days after the crime. Dr. Harwell had withdrawn one hundred and twenty thousand dollars, the full amount of her personal checking and savings accounts.

A low whistle escaped Josh's lips. Dr. Cassandra Harwell was one tough shrew. He looked at her picture again. Not the typical face of a born killer, but she did look a little uptight—kind of the way Chrysie had looked the other night when she'd lit into him about the crooked Christmas tree.

But not the way she'd looked serving up plates of sloppy joes and washing dishes in her cozy little kitchen. Definitely not the way she'd looked when she'd stood at the back door to tell them goodbye. Her vulnerability then had really gotten to him. Of course, she could have been playing him.

He studied the picture again. Different color and hairstyle. That was easy enough to accomplish. Chrysie was shapely where the woman in the picture was too thin, but a few added pounds could explain that.

And there were some very definite similarities. The shape of the face was the same and the features were similar. Little turned-up nose, full lips. And something about the eyes. The similarities didn't justify tearing out to the Millers' ranch to make an arrest, but when you considered the two children were exactly the right ages, there was ample evidence to warrant further investigation.

If Chrysie was the missing psychologist, it would explain her Texas accent and the way she knew so much about handling the boys. It would also explain why she could be a stay-at-home mom. She could still be making it on the one-twenty if she'd lived as cheaply the past three years as she was now.

He should be feeling at least a hint of excitement

at the possibility of arresting a fugitive practically in his backyard. Instead he felt more as if he'd taken a punch to the gut. His muscles tightened as he picked up the phone and dialed information for the phone number for the Houston Police Department. With any luck, he'd find the listing was a mistake and that Dr. Cassandra Harwell had been located months ago.

He had a very strong hunch that this was not his lucky day.

DETECTIVE JUAN HERNANDEZ hung up the phone and lumbered down the hall to his new partner's office. Her door was open, so he walked in. Angela Martina was sitting at her desk, her breasts pushing ever so slightly against the soft cotton of her yellow blouse as she shuffled through the photos of last night's shooting on the east side of town.

"Lousy photos," she said. "I may have to start taking my own."

He looked at the photo she'd just thrown to her desk. It looked fine to him. "I just got a call from a sheriff in Aohkii, Montana," he said.

She didn't bother to look up. "What's his problem?"

"He was calling about Cassandra Harwell." He knew that would get her attention. Jonathan Harwell and Angela's older sister had been partners in a law firm before he was murdered.

Angela tossed the photo she was holding back to

the desk and stared at Juan from beneath her mascara-coated lashes. "Has Cassandra been spotted in Montana?"

"Probably not. Said he had some strangers in town and he was checking them against known felons."

"I don't guess the strangers are a woman with two small children?"

"He said there were some children. He'd check and see if they matched the ages of the Harwell kids."

"Did he give you a description of the woman?"

"No, only said she didn't much favor the online photo of Cassandra Harwell."

"So why did he call?"

"You know those Montana guys. What else they got to do up there besides cozy up to a sheep?" He laughed at his own joke. Angela didn't.

"What did you tell him?" she asked.

"To check out the kids. If the woman had two girls that looked anywhere near the ages of the Harwell kids, he should get us a set of fingerprints from the woman and keep an eye on her until we checked them out."

"Did he agree to cooperate?"

"Yeah. Said no problem. He seems on top of things, but I don't look for anything to come of this. I can't see Cassandra in Montana. More likely she's down in Mexico somewhere. No reason to be freezing her ass off up there."

Angela drummed her bright red nails on her desk. "If it's Cassandra, someone from the department will need to go up there and fly her back. Frankly I would love to see some snow. It's hard to get in the mood for Christmas shopping when I'm still running the air conditioner."

"Well, don't make any plane reservations just yet. This is a really long shot."

"Just keep me posted." Angela turned her gaze back to the photos.

Juan lingered. "You want to get some breakfast and then go question the usual suspects on the east side?"

"Not if we have to go to that greasy hole-in-the-wall where we went last time."

"They make good breakfast tacos."

"I want a bagel. And give me a few minutes. I have to make a phone call before we go."

He started to drop into the straight-backed chair near her desk to wait.

"A *private* phone call."

He grinned and left, though he'd love to hang around and listen. Angela was single and the hottest number on the force. He could imagine what a private phone call from her would sound like. Not that he'd ever get one. She'd made it clear she didn't date police officers. He guessed that meant she wouldn't sleep with him either.

He walked back to his office, once again thinking

about the sheriff's call. Be one great boon if it was
Cassandra Harwell who'd shown up in Aohkii, Montana. He was as eager as ever to get his hands on the
murdering bitch—for reasons that had nothing to do
with her husband's death.

JENNY GATHERED a handful of snow and hurled it in
her mother's direction. The snowball splattered
against the leg of Chrysie's jeans. "Okay, kid, you're
going to get it now."

Jenny took off running, her boots sinking in the
snow with each step. Chrysie caught her easily,
grabbed her around the waist and swung her around
while Jenny squealed excitedly.

Mandy came running over. "Swing me, too,
Mommy."

"As soon as I catch my breath." She took a huge
gulp of the cold air, marveling again at how gloriously
beautiful the world looked covered in white. Last
night's snowfall had been the heaviest of the season
and had left the entire mountainside glistening.

It was one more reason she'd love to stay in
Aohkii. Actually, she'd love to stay almost anywhere.
Constantly moving from one town to another was
hard on her and even worse on the girls.

Every town they settled in seemed to have its
drawbacks. At least it had seemed that way until
she'd arrived in Aohkii one sunny afternoon two

months ago. She'd only planned to stop for lunch, but when she'd heard some young mothers at a nearby table talking about the excellent preschool program at the Methodist church, her interest had been piqued.

And then when she'd followed up on the waitress's suggestion that she contact the Millers about renting their cabin, she'd felt it was meant to be, had even dared to hope they could make a real life here.

But now she had Sheriff Josh McCain to deal with. If his questions and interest in her persisted, she'd have no choice but to run again. Her heart constricted at the thought of tearing her innocent daughters away from this place that seemed so perfect.

She picked up Mandy and spun her around until she grew so dizzy she had to lean against the trunk of a towering tree for support. Mandy needed no recuperation.

"Look, Mommy. I'm making snow angels," she announced as she flopped around in the snow like an injured bird.

"That's not how you do it." Jenny fell to her back and started demonstrating the correct way—not that Mandy was looking at her. Mandy had already given up on snow angels and was standing and brushing the snow from her bright red parka. She wandered a few feet away, then came back and grabbed Chrysie's hand. "Come see this, Mommy."

"Yes. The spruce tree looks very pretty covered in snow."

"It's not a 'pruce tree. It's a Christmas tree."

"I guess it could be."

"Can we have it for our tree? Can we, please? I love it."

Jenny jumped up from the snow and came over to voice her protest. "It's not tall enough to be a Christmas tree."

"They don't have to be tall, do they, Mommy?"

"I'm pretty sure there's no height requirement."

"What's height?" Mandy asked.

"That's how you measure how tall something is."

"I want lots of height," Jenny said, "for the decorations. And we can put a big star on top, just like the one on the tree in *The Night Before Christmas*."

"I want this tree," Mandy insisted.

"There's no law against having two Christmas trees," Chrysie said. "Maybe we can leave the small one outside so that it can keep growing. We can decorate it for the birds so that they won't go hungry for Christmas."

"Two Christmas trees." Jenny was clearly impressed.

The hum of an engine grabbed Chrysie's attention, and she turned to see a truck making its way up the center of the freshly plowed road that led from the highway. She expected it to be Buck Miller or one of his hands, but as the vehicle got closer, her heart plunged to her toes. It was Sheriff McCain.

She grew instantly tense, starting the all-too-familiar acid flow to her stomach and constricting her throat so that it was difficult to swallow.

No reason to panic, she told herself. *He's just here to see the Millers. Or else he wants me to watch the boys for him. If he asks, I'll say yes. Pretend it's no problem. Pretend* he's *no problem.*

She waved and managed a smile as he stopped a few feet from them and stepped out of his truck. It struck her how well he fit in this world of snowy isolation and rugged terrain.

"Good morning," she said, striving to sound at ease. "Back so soon?"

"That's what happens when you feed a stray. They just keep hanging around until you run them off with a well-placed broom handle."

"Lucky me, I have a new broom." She turned back to the girls as he joined them. "Time to go inside and warm up."

"Don't go in on my account," Josh said. "I didn't come to visit. I was heading up to the Millers' house to talk to Buck about some cattle he's selling, but I saw you and the girls outside and wondered if you were having battery trouble again."

"No, I have a new one."

"Good thinking. Guess you just decided to give

the girls a holiday. I don't blame you. I was tempted to let the boys stay home, but once they hit first grade, the teachers frown on that."

"I assumed school would be called off due to the weather."

"It's just a little snow. Plows already have the main roads cleared. And looks like Buck took care of this one."

"Yes. One of his hands was out just after daybreak."

Jenny marched to the back door, sinking her boots as far as she could into the mounds of snow. Mandy ran over and shoved her small gloved hand in Josh's much larger one. "I can make snow angels. You wanna watch me?"

"Of course I do." He raved over her abilities as she fell to her back and did a repeat of her flapping-arms routine.

Chrysie worked on staying outwardly calm as she watched the sheriff bond with her young daughter. It seemed a natural thing to do, yet it filled her with dread.

"I didn't come to visit," he said again, "but since I'm here, I sure could use a cup of coffee."

"Sure," she said. "I can make a fresh pot."

Josh swooped Mandy onto his shoulders and started toward the back door. Chrysie's legs felt leaden as she followed them inside.

JOSH STUDIED CHRYSIE'S every move as she helped the girls out of their snow pants, parkas and boots. They were happy kids. She clearly adored them. Which didn't mean a damn thing. Danny and Davy's mother had probably loved them, too, but it hadn't kept her from living in a world so depraved he didn't even like to think about it.

Mandy pulled off her mittens and held her hands out in front of her. "They're still cold."

Chrysie held them in hers for a second. "How about some hot chocolate to warm you up?"

"With marshmallows?" Mandy asked.

"Marshmallows and a cookie, just as soon as I get the coffee started."

Josh hung his jacket on one of the hooks near the back door. "Actually, the hot chocolate sounds good."

"Then it's hot chocolate all around."

Josh had given little thought to how he'd handle this, mostly trusting his instincts to guide the conversation while he asked enough questions to give him a feel for whether or not Chrysie was on the run.

He watched as she measured cocoa, sugar and milk and dumped the ingredients into a small saucepan. "I didn't know anyone still made hot chocolate the old-fashioned way."

"I don't always. I have instant on hand, as well."

"So what's the special occasion?"

"Snow."

"I guess you didn't get much of that back in—where was it you're from? Texas?"

"No." She kept her back to him. "Actually, I'm from Mississippi, but I haven't lived there since graduating college. My husband and I moved around a lot."

"Was that because of his job?"

"Right."

"What kind of business was he in?"

"He was a helicopter pilot with the Army."

"I had some friends who flew helicopters for the Army."

He would.

"Where did your husband do his training?"

"In…in Alabama. Near Mobile."

"Really? I didn't know there was an Army base there."

"No, you're right. It wasn't Alabama. It was somewhere in…in south Texas. I don't know where. It was before we were married."

The question had her flustered. He walked to the counter so that he could see her face while she worked. "How long has he been dead?"

"Almost three years. Mandy was just a baby. Jennifer was only two." Finally she looked up and met his gaze. "I don't like talking about this, Sheriff. My husband's death was a very unhappy time in my life that I'm trying to put behind me."

"I can understand that. I'm sorry I asked." He

was—and becoming more disturbed by the second. This wasn't just about Chrysie. It was about Jenny and Mandy and what would happen to them if their mother wound up in jail. They'd be faced with the same kind of trauma Danny and Davy had dealt with, except there wouldn't be a father to step in and love them.

"How many Christmas trees are you going to have?" Mandy asked.

"One."

"We're going to have two. One for the birds and one with a big star."

"Boy, two trees. That's pretty cool." So Mandy was three, Jenny was five—exactly the same ages the Harwell girls would be. If Chrysie was on the run, she should have lied about that, but that would have meant having her girls confused about their ages and starting them in school at the wrong age. She was probably too good a mother for that.

Chrysie filled two cups when the chocolate was little more than lukewarm. She waited until it was steaming to fill the other two colorful pottery mugs. Each cup received two fluffy marshmallows. The girls got a sugar cookie with their drink. He got a piece of nuked pie. He forked a bite when they'd all sat down at the kitchen table, though he'd lost his appetite.

"Are you going to Mississippi to see your grandparents for Christmas, Jenny, or are you going to stay up here and have a white Christmas with us?"

"My grandma and grandpa are in heaven with my dad," Jenny said, "so we can't visit them."

Josh wondered if the grandparents were really dead or if that was part of the altered reality of a woman on the run.

"You were great with the boys yesterday," Josh said, deciding to take a different path with his questioning. "You would have made a great teacher."

"I doubt I have the patience for that."

"What was your major?"

"My major?"

"Yeah, in college. You said you didn't leave Mississippi until after you got your degree."

She hesitated way too long, and her hands tightened on her cup as if she thought it might jump off the table if she didn't hold it down. She was saved by Mandy when she accidentally knocked over her drink, sending a river of chocolate across the table.

"It's okay," Chrysie said as she jumped up to get a handful of paper towels. "Accidents happen."

"Some gotted on my pants," Mandy said.

"And all over my hands," Jenny said.

"Okay, everybody to the bathroom. Will you excuse us, Sheriff?"

"Absolutely." Josh waited until they were out of sight before walking to the counter and using two fingers to pick up the measuring cup Chrysie had used for the milk. He'd watched and knew it would have a good set of fingerprints and figured she'd be less likely to miss it than one of her pretty cups. Careful not to smudge the prints, he slipped it into the plastic zip bag he'd brought with him.

He stashed it in the pocket of his jacket and went back to his pie and chocolate. When Chrysie returned, it was just to stick her head in the doorway.

"I hate to be a terrible hostess, but I need to get these clothes off to soak before the stains become permanent."

She smiled, but it didn't reach her deep blue eyes. When he stared into their smoky depths, he saw the same vulnerability that had gotten to him last night.

"That's okay. I need to get a move on myself. Thanks for the pie and chocolate."

"You're welcome."

He couldn't actually feel the weight of the cup in his pocket as he left, but he was intensely aware of it as he climbed behind the wheel of his truck. He hoped to hell the prints were not those of Cassandra Harwell.

Yet he was almost certain that they were. And just as certain that arresting her might top his list of the hardest things he'd ever had to do.

CHRYSIE'S HEART WAS pounding like mad as she watched the truck disappear down the road, not toward the Millers but back to the highway.

He knew. She was sure of it.

The references to Texas. The questions about her husband's helicopter training, her parents and her education. And the missing measuring cup. He'd probably though she wouldn't notice. He was wrong. She hadn't avoided capture for three years by letting anything go unnoticed.

He had her fingerprints, and as soon as he had them tested, he'd be back to arrest her. She had to move quickly, had only hours, maybe minutes, to throw what she could into the car. Only moments to tear the girls away from the place they already thought of as home.

Tears burned at the back of her eyelids as she hurried to her bedroom and pulled the battered suitcases from the top shelf of the closet. She carried two to the girls' room. Her hands flew as she packed their socks, undies and pajamas, hoping to finish before they wandered in and saw what she was doing.

Better to get them in the car and on the road without their knowing what was going on. That way they couldn't say anything to anyone when they stopped at a service station for fuel or at a fast-food restaurant for a bite to eat.

She had no idea where they'd go now. Before, she'd always known, but this time she hadn't been able to make herself think of that next move. Aohkii had seemed so perfect.

She took the suitcases to the back door, then went to the living room, where the girls were watching cartoons and coloring pictures in their new drawing pads. "I have a surprise for you," she said, trying to keep her tone light. "We're going on a little trip."

Mandy jumped off the couch. "Are we going to get a heighted Christmas tree?"

"Not heighted, tall," Jenny corrected. "Are we, Mommy?"

"Not yet, but we'll have fun. We'll be riding in the car for a while, so I want you to go to your room and pick out five toys you want to take with you."

The crayon Jenny was using slipped from her fingers and rolled along the table before falling to the floor. She stared at Chrysie questioningly. "What about the Christmas play? We have to go to practice."

"The next practice isn't until Monday. We'll be back by then." She hated lying to Jenny. Hated that she had to let her believe they'd be coming back when they never would. But she simply couldn't take a chance on Jenny saying anything until they were far away from Aohkii.

"I don't want to go."

Chrysie settled on the couch beside Jenny and put her arm around her thin shoulders. "It will be okay, sweetheart. I promise you we'll have fun." She touched her lips to the top of Jenny's head and felt the wispy strands of hair against her face.

"I don't want to move again, Mommy. I like it in Aohkii."

Chrysie pulled her close. "We don't have a lot of time, Jenny. Just go to your room and pick out five toys. I'll explain everything later."

Chrysie wanted to hate Josh McCain, wanted to blame him for all this unhappiness and pain, but she couldn't. Her own mistakes had caused this. Mistakes that she could never undo.

All she could do now was hope to outrun the killers and the law.

CHRYSIE WAS TWENTY miles east of Aohkii when she heard the approaching police siren. Impulsively she pressed her foot onto the accelerator.

Seconds later, the car hit an icy spot and started to skid. The back end of the car fishtailed to the right. Chrysie fought the wheel to straighten the car, but they were going sideways now, skidding toward the ditch and a cluster of pine trees just off the road.

The girls started to scream. She started to pray. But the horrifying siren just kept wailing right through the deafening crash.

Chapter Four

Josh hit the brakes and jumped from his truck, cursing the snow that slowed his steps as he rushed to the wrecked car. Panic and guilt whirled in a rush of adrenaline. This was his fault. He should have handled the situation better, should have confronted Chrysie at the house instead of waiting to catch her when she made a run for it.

He could hear crying as he approached the car. He jerked open the back door. Mandy was still in her car seat but sobbing. Jenny was unbuckling her own seat belt while trying to comfort her little sister.

"Don't cry, Mandy. We're okay."

Mandy's sobs slowed to a whimper at the sight of Josh. The girls appeared to be unhurt. Chrysie was a different story. She wasn't moving, and her head was leaning against the blood-smeared side window.

"It's okay, girls," Josh said. "I'm here and I'll take care of everything." He didn't feel nearly that confident as he tried to open the front door of the car only to find it so jammed from the wreck that it didn't budge. He raced around the car to the passenger-side door, and Chrysie groaned and opened her eyes as he slid in beside her.

"Mandy and Jenny?"

"They're fine," he said.

Chrysie twisted to see for herself. Both girls were out of their car seats now and leaning against the front seat.

"You're bleeding, Mommy." Jenny's small voice quivered, and that sent another shot of guilt straight to Josh's heart. Not only could he have killed them all in a stupid car chase, he was still about to rip their mother from them.

"I'm okay, sweetie." Chrysie's voice was slurred, and when she turned back to Josh her eyes were clouded with confusion.

A trickle of blood ran down her right temple and dripped onto her shirt. She reached up and ran her fingers across a knot just above her ear that had already swelled to the size of golf ball.

"I was..." Reality apparently kicked in, halting her words. She started to shake. "Don't do this, Josh."

His throat went dry. Arresting her shouldn't be this damn hard.

"It's not what it seems," she whispered. "It's not." She looked back at the girls, and he could have sworn he could hear the splintering sounds of her heart breaking.

"I'm sorry, Chrysie, but you're under…" He looked into her eyes. They seemed to be miles deep, all mist and pain—and pleading.

"I didn't do it. Just let us go and I'll be out of your life and out of your county."

She made it sound so simple. It wasn't. "It's out of my hands."

"No. It's in your hands. We're in your hands—me and Jenny and Mandy."

She moaned softly and her head fell against his shoulder. She jerked it away only to let it fall to the back of the seat. Her eyes were rolling about in her head now and she was incredibly pale.

"My mommy's hurt," Jenny said. "She needs to go see the doctor. You have to help her."

From the mouths of babes. "You're right. She needs a doctor." He slipped his arm around Chrysie's shoulders while he called for an ambulance. He didn't have a doubt in the world at this point that she'd lied about who she was. She was Cassandra Harwell, a wanted woman.

But he couldn't bring himself to cuff her in front of the girls, especially not in her condition. She'd been on the run for three years. Another few hours wasn't going to make that much difference.

"If she goes to the hospital, who's going to take care of us?" Mandy asked.

"Don't you worry about that. I've got everything under control," he lied.

Mandy reached over from the backseat, stretched her short arms around his neck and planted a kiss on his ear. "Thank you, Mr. Sheriff."

Yeah, Sheriff Judas, saying all the right things while he made plans to ruin their lives in the name of the law. But then, what choice did he have?

IT TOOK TWELVE stitches to close the wound in Chrysie's head. It hadn't been all that deep, but it had stretched from an inch or two inside the hairline down the temple, apparently caused by one of the girls' toys that had flown into the front seat and gotten caught between Chrysie's head and the window during the wild skidding.

Cougar, Josh's friend and sometimes deputy, had checked out the scene of the wreck. He'd reported that the vehicle had been slowed by the mounds of snow left by the plow that morning, easing the impact and likely saving the occupants' lives.

Josh hadn't left the hospital, hadn't even left Chrysie's bedside except when they'd taken the patient for X-rays and when the nurse had sent him out so she could undress Chrysie and get her into a hospital gown.

She'd given her name as Chrysie Atwater when she'd checked in. He hadn't protested. Truth was, he still thought of her that way, almost as if his emotions were overriding his mind. And therein lay most of his problems.

The consensus of medical opinion was that she had a mild concussion but that there were no serious external or internal injuries. A couple of days' rest and she should be as good as new. The bruises on her arms and legs would take a little longer to disappear.

Josh had called Evelyn Miller, and she'd come to stay with the girls while they were examined. Once they had been declared in good shape, Evelyn had insisted that she take the girls and his sons home with her for the night.

Chrysie moved her arms from beneath the covers. He had the crazy urge to take her hand. He fought it for a second, then gave in when she moaned as if in pain.

She opened her eyes, blinked a few times and squinted as she turned to face him. "Where are my girls?"

"With Evelyn. They're fine."

"Are you sure they're okay?"

"They both had thorough examinations, and the doctor said there were no injuries, not even minor ones."

"Did you tell Evelyn about me?"

"I haven't told anyone."

She ran her tongue over her dry lips. He poured a glass of water from the pitcher by her bed, then slipped his right arm beneath her shoulders to help her raise enough to sip from the straw.

She drank, then let her head fall back to the pillow. "I didn't kill him, Josh."

He hadn't planned to get into this so soon, but there wasn't much way to avoid it now that she'd brought it up. "If you were innocent, why did you run?"

"To save them."

"To save who?"

"Jenny and Mandy." Her eyes seemed haunted, as if they were mirroring an unspeakable horror. "He would have killed them."

The intensity of her fear filled the room. He hated to even think what the man might have done to instill a terror that had remained this intense for three years. "He's dead, Chrysie. Your husband is dead. He can't hurt you or the girls anymore."

"Jonathan's dead, but his killer isn't."

The nurse knocked once and then came into the room. Josh stood and walked to the window, staring out into the brilliance of Montana sunlight on a frosted world while the nurse checked Chrysie's pulse and temperature. Old memories claimed his mind, going back to his days in New Orleans. He'd never played by the rules back then, never lived by anyone's code but his own.

He was still standing at the window when the E.R. physician who'd treated Chrysie stepped into the room. The nurse handed him Chrysie's chart. He studied it for a few seconds, then pulled a chair up to Chrysie's bed.

"How do you feel?" he asked.

"I'm okay."

"You're lucky, that's for sure. It's always nice to walk away from a serious automobile accident with no more than a few stitches and a mild concussion."

"Yeah, lucky."

"So how do you really feel? And don't play tough with me. I'm the doctor, I'm supposed to hear your complaints."

"I'm a little stiff," she admitted.

"I'm afraid that's going to continue and probably get worse over the next few days. I'd like you to stay in the hospital tonight for observation. But if all goes well—and I see no reason it shouldn't—you can go home in the morning."

"I can't stay."

The doctor was busy making notes on Chrysie's chart. He didn't look up. "And why is it you can't stay?"

"I have two daughters."

"I saw the neighbor who came to pick them up. They appeared to be in good hands."

"It's been a traumatic day. I need to be with them."

"What you need is rest, but I'll check in with you

later, and we'll talk about the possibility of your going home tonight."

As soon as the nurse and the doctor left, Chrysie pushed to a very shaky sitting position and started looking around the room. "Where are my clothes?"

"Where do you think you're going?"

"We have to talk, Josh, but not here. And I'm not going anywhere in this hospital gown."

Josh knew he should start reciting the Miranda rights about now. The first sentence rolled through his brain but got nowhere near his lips. He took a deep breath and exhaled slowly. "Okay, we'll talk, but it will be on my terms."

Chrysie trembled. He wasn't sure if she was afraid or thankful. It didn't much matter. He couldn't make any promises.

He dropped to the chair by her bed and took her shaking hands in his. They were cold as ice. "We can talk later," he said. "Right now, just try to rest, like the doctor said."

She closed her eyes, and he thought she might have drifted off when he heard her whisper sluggishly. "I didn't kill Jonathan."

It was downright scary how badly he wanted to believe her.

JOSH PACED HIS SMALL kitchen in the wee hours of the morning, wishing now he hadn't drunk so much of the strong hospital coffee as the afternoon had stretched into the early hours of the evening. It was after six before Chrysie had been released, making it near seven by the time they'd gotten back to Aohkii.

Chrysie had either slept or faked sleep most of the ride home. Josh was pretty sure it was the latter since her muscles had seemed too taut to be at rest. But she'd been fully animated as they'd approached the edge of town, had insisted they stop at the Millers' and pick up Jenny and Mandy.

He'd given in only after he'd realized that doing what Chrysie said or shooting her were his only two options. So here he was with a murder suspect he hadn't arrested as yet and four children under the age of seven.

Fortunately Buck had offered to temporarily exchange his SUV for Josh's pickup. And the always thoughtful Evelyn had fed the kids before he and Chrysie had arrived and had packed a doggie bag of vegetable-beef soup and fresh-baked bread for him and Chrysie. Supper had been a breeze. Bedtime had been an ordeal straight from hell.

The four children had fought not over the two bunk beds but over who got to sleep on the mats on the floor in the den. So they were all in there now, spread out across the den floor so that there was hardly room to place his size-eleven feet between them—and that was the only path from his bedroom to the kitchen.

Not that he needed to get into his bedroom, since that was where Chrysie was sleeping. That left bunk beds for him, another reason he was wandering around in the kitchen in the middle of the night. He couldn't sleep in a bed that made him feel like a third-grader on a sleepover.

Oh, who the hell was he kidding? He couldn't sleep because of the tormenting thoughts roaming about in his head like a bunch of lost sheep. No matter how many spins he put on the situation, it didn't change the fact that he was aiding and abetting a fugitive from justice. At the very least, he should have notified the Houston Police Department that Cassandra Harwell and her two children were in his custody.

And he would—first thing in the morning. If she was innocent, she could hire an attorney and prove it. That's the way the law worked.

Only… He jumped to attention as he heard a bump in the den. He crossed the room and pushed the door open. Chrysie was maneuvering the quilts, pillows, arms and legs and had apparently stubbed her toe on the leg of the old pine coffee table that he'd pushed into one corner.

Her mouth twisted into a jumble of weird faces as she hopped her way toward him. She didn't moan until she fell into one of the kitchen chairs and pulled her foot into her lap so she could cradle the ailing little toe.

"Guess I should have warned you about the wall-to-wall kids," he said.

"Don't you have beds?"

"No, but then I hadn't really planned on using the cabin as a resort."

"Or a jail," she said, bringing everything back into perspective as she dropped her foot back to the floor. She looked around the small kitchen as if seeing it for the first time, though she'd had a few bites of Evelyn's soup there a few hours earlier.

"Can I get you something?" he asked. "Water? Juice?"

"Juice would be good."

He poured her a glass, then joined her at the table, feeling about as awkward as a man could get in his own kitchen. He watched as she took a slow sip of the juice, then washed her lips with the tip of her tongue. With another woman, he might have thought it was a purposely seductive act, but the troubled look in Chrysie's eyes and the worried wrinkles around her eyes were proof she had much more serious thoughts on her mind.

She set the glass on the table and looked up, locking her gaze with his. "We have to talk."

"That can wait until morning."

"No, it can't."

"Then I should read you your rights and let you know that anything you say might be held against you."

"Don't bother. The only right I'm worried about is the right to live and keep my daughters safe."

Damn. She sure knew how to get to him, especially since he'd been in that same spot not so long ago. He leaned back in the chair and crossed his ankle over his knee, suddenly aware the cozy scene the two of them presented. He was barefoot and bare-chested, dressed only in a pair of faded jeans and an open flannel shirt. She was wearing a pair of blue-and-white polka-dot pajamas that he'd rummaged from the luggage his deputy had had the good sense to pull from her wrecked car before it was towed.

A defense attorney worth his salt would have a field day with this scenario for questioning between a sheriff and a suspect. But it was a little late to worry about legalities and proprieties now.

"I didn't kill my husband," she said. "We had an argument, and I took the girls and stormed out of the house, but I didn't kill him."

"So who did?"

"I don't know."

Chrysie knotted and unknotted her hands. Guilty people did that sometimes when they were lying during questioning. But then, scared people did it, too. He'd always been good telling the difference, but none of his usual objectiveness held true with Chrysie.

"What did you and your husband argue about the night he was murdered?"

"I'd just found out that he was sleeping with his secretary."

Josh swallowed hard. Talk about your classic motive. But the man had to be crazy to give at the office if he had Chrysie Atwater waiting at home.

Only she wasn't Chrysie Atwater, and he'd best start getting that straight.

CHRYSIE HAD BATTLED and beaten the odds for three years, but it had all caught up with her now. The night was eerily quiet, with no sounds except the wind's low moaning and the occasional creak that was part of every old house. And the scrape of Josh's chair on the worn linoleum as he pulled himself closer to the table.

"How much do you know about me?" she asked.

"I know you're a child psychologist and that you came home early in the morning after spending the night in a hotel and found your husband murdered in his bed. I know you withdrew all your available cash and fled the area. Is that accurate?"

"It's true but not really accurate."

"So why don't you tell me your version?"

She took a deep breath. "We argued that night. I accused him of having an affair with his secretary. He exploded but denied it. Bottom line is that I took the girls and spent the night in a Houston hotel."

"And you stayed there all night?"

"No." This was where things got sticky, where the lies had started. "I told the police I'd arrived home at eight the next morning, but that wasn't exactly the truth. Mandy was only three months old. She woke during the night with colic, and when I couldn't quiet her, I decided to go home so that I could give her some of the medication her pediatrician had prescribed."

"Why did you lie about the timing?"

She took a deep breath. "I'll get to that. It's complicated, Josh."

"Murder usually is."

"I parked the car in the garage at a few minutes after three in the morning. Mandy had fallen asleep on the ride home, so I carried her in first and put her in her crib. Then I went back for Jenny. I had planned to sleep on the sofa, but I saw the light shining through the crack beneath the bedroom door and thought Jonathan was still awake."

The memories were pummeling her mind now, sickening, bloody memories that knotted in her stomach and scraped along every nerve ending. "I opened the bedroom door, and that's when I saw my husband's body. Lying on his back. With a bullet through his head."

Josh murmured a curse. She didn't look up, didn't want to meet his gaze and see doubt in his eyes. She had to get through this, had to make him understand why she'd run—and why she couldn't go back.

"I don't know how long I stood there. I thought it was a second, but it could have been longer. I'm not sure if the man said something or if I just felt his presence and looked behind me. But he was there, standing in the door, smiling as if this were all a joke."

"So you're saying you saw the killer?"

"Killers. There were two of them, though I didn't know that until a few minutes later."

"Is this what you told the police?"

"No."

"Why not?"

"Because they said if I did, they'd kill my babies."

"So go back to where we were. You were in the bedroom when a man came in. What happened next?"

"He put a gun to my head and marched me into the living room. The other man was there, on the landing, dangling Mandy over the banister as if he were going to drop her."

"But he didn't drop her?"

"No, but he was laughing and saying how much fun it would be to kill her. The other man said that I was to tell the police I had just come in and found Jonathan dead. He said that if I mentioned them at all, they'd be back and they'd kill all three of us." Finally she looked up and into Josh's gaze. "They would have killed us, Josh, and they still will. That's why I can't go to the police."

"The police will protect you and the girls."

"Would you be willing to take that chance with Danny and Davy?"

He didn't answer. She prayed that meant he understood. "Let me go, Josh. I'm begging you, for the sake of the girls if not for me. Just let us walk away and forget you ever saw us."

"I'm afraid I can't do that."

Chrysie wouldn't have hesitated for a second to strangle him with her bare hands if she thought she could do it. She'd risked it all, told him the truth, and now he was ready to turn against her and hand that information to the police.

She jumped to her feet and stared down at him. "If Mandy and Jenny are harmed, it will be your doing. Are you willing to live with that, Sheriff Josh McCain?"

He stood, as well, and put his hands on her shoulders. "Calm down, Chrysie. You'll wake the kids."

"If you care anything at all about my daughters, you won't send us back to Houston."

"I won't send you back to Houston, at least not until I have time to check this out. But I'm not letting you run away again, either. You'll have to stay here."

"In Aohkii?"

"In Aohkii and in this house."

"You mean as a prisoner?"

"That's not the way I'd put it, but it pretty much sums it up. If I find out you've lied to me or if you try to escape, I'll fly you to Houston myself. Is that clear?"

"Perfectly clear." She'd be in this house with one bathroom and four kids. In this house with only one double bed and two bunks. In this house with a man who made her remember she was a woman.

"Good. Now that we have that settled, let's go to bed."

Chapter Five

—

"Danny knocked over his juice," Jenny squealed, jumping from her chair in time to miss the river of sticky beverage headed her way.

Josh dropped the unopened carton of milk on the counter and lunged for paper towels. He absorbed what he could as the rest puddled around Danny's plate or dripped onto the worn linoleum.

"No more horseplay at the table," Josh said, though he had no idea how the accident had actually happened. He opened the milk and set it in the middle of the rectangular table along with three boxes of cereal. "Take your pick."

Jenny climbed back in her chair and reached for the cereal, turning each box around so that she could see the front of it. "Our mom doesn't let us eat those," she announced. "They have too much sugar in them."

"Sorry, it's all I have."

"Then Mandy and I have to have something else for breakfast."

Mandy reached for one of the boxes. "I like sugar."

Davy scooted his chair back and hopped down from the table.

Josh stepped in front of him. "Where do you think you're going?"

"I've gotta go pee."

"Well, make it snappy—and wash your hands."

"My mom always gives us two choices for breakfast," Jenny announced.

But Supermom was still asleep, and Josh wasn't about to wake her. She needed her rest. He did, too, for that matter. He didn't have a concussion, but the last twenty-four hours had definitely been traumatic.

Mandy's spoon went clattering to the floor. Josh handed her another, then poured himself a cup of strong black coffee. By the time he got back to the table, Danny's hand and forearm had disappeared into a box of cereal and sugarcoated puffs were spilling out and bouncing around the table.

"What's wrong with the cereal at the top of the box?" Josh asked.

"I'm looking for the prize."

Danny appeared at that moment, hands dripping. "Hey, I'm supposed to get the prize this time."

"Uh-uh." Davy pulled a plastic dinosaur from the

box and held it up, taunting his brother. "You got the last prize."

"Didn't count. It was that stupid dancing pig, and I threw it away."

"Then you just lost your turn."

"Eat," Josh said, "or the dinosaur goes in the trash."

"I don't have anything to eat," Jenny said.

"Right. You want choices. How about a scrambled egg or toast and jelly?"

Mandy started crying. Josh rushed back to the table. "What's wrong?"

"Davy threw his dinosaur in my cereal."

"It was an accident. I was just pitching it up in the air and it fell in."

"Give me the dinosaur," Josh demanded. He tossed it to the counter and put a hand on Mandy's shoulder. "The dinosaur's gone. Do you want some toast and jelly, too?"

"No, I want my mommy."

She'd quit crying, but she was still sniffing and looking as if she might start again at any moment. Nothing scared Josh more than a female's tears—a secret that he didn't want out. "Your mother's asleep, Mandy, but as soon as she wakes up, you can go in the bedroom and see her."

"Is she still sick?"

"She's better. She just needs rest."

"Who's going to take me to kindergarten?" Jenny demanded.

"No one. It's Saturday." And that might be the only good thing about any of this. He'd never have gotten the four of them dressed and into town by eight.

"I don't like eggs, so what kind of jelly do you have?" Jenny asked.

"Grape and strawberry."

"I like grape."

Josh's cell phone rang. He rescued it from beneath a dish towel and checked the caller ID. It was his brother Logan in New Orleans. He started to ignore the ring, but he could use some of Logan's sage advice about now, and the guy was harder to get hold of than a used-car salesman after the deal.

"Okay, kids, keep it quiet—and eat."

He pushed though the storm door and onto the back porch before answering. "Hello, Logan."

"How are things in Montana?"

"Great, unless you're bothered by youthful chaos, flying cereal and rivers of orange juice." And women wanted for murder sleeping in your bed.

"Sounds as if the boys are in top form."

"Masters of the game."

"Good, they're really why I called. Rachel wants to make a fast trip your way before the Christmas holidays. She says she wants to see holiday snow, but I can tell she misses Danny and Davy."

"That's not a good idea."

"Don't tell me you have problems up there in cowboy country?"

"Complications."

"That sounds very suspicious. These complications wouldn't involve a woman, would they?"

"You know me too well."

"So have you met someone new? Is this serious?"

"Let's just say it's…complicated."

"You already said that."

Josh peeked inside the back door. Things were reasonably under control—*reasonably* meaning there were no food fights or overturned furniture. And no tears.

"It's a long story and I don't have much time," Josh said, "so listen carefully." He told the story as briefly as he could.

"Let me see if I have this straight," Logan said. "You have moved a woman wanted for suspicion of murder into your house."

"Believe me, she's no murderous psychopath, if that's what you're thinking. And she'll only be here long enough for me to see if her story checks out."

"And just how would you verify this since the only people who know if she's telling the truth are her dead husband and the two men she *claimed* killed him?"

"I have ways. Look, I know her story sounds fishy, but…"

"You think? She finds out her husband is running around on her and that same night two men she's never heard of just happen to come by and shoot him right before she walks in the house."

"It could happen."

"Sure it could. Now let me guess. The woman is coyote-ugly with tiny breasts and her face is covered in warts."

"Okay, so she's good-looking, but that's not what this is about. She's scared, Logan, really scared, and not for herself. She's scared for her daughters. I don't know, maybe it's because Tess put our sons into so much danger, but the fact that she's such a dedicated mother gets to me. And I'm not going to let some D.A. in Houston decide how I do my job."

"You were always one to make your own rules, but just be careful. And if there's anything I can do, let me know."

"I may take you up on that, little brother. Oops, got to go. My two loving sons require a referee."

CHRYSIE AWOKE TO squeals and the kind of clattering you'd expect if the back half of the cabin were being demolished. She sat up in bed to the protest of a stiff neck and a headache. Ignoring them, she threw her legs over the side of the bed and staggered to the kitchen.

"Mommy, you're up." Mandy wrapped herself around Chrysie's legs.

Chrysie bent, gave her a reassuring hug, then studied the scene in front of her. Jenny was standing by the table, arms folded, while Danny and Davy were going at each other with feet and arms flying.

Josh was storming through the back door, looking aggravated and incredibly virile. His dark hair was rumpled, and thick locks of it had fallen over his brow. And the sleeves of his pale yellow Western shirt were pushed up, revealing a scattering of dark hairs on his sun-bronzed arms.

He grabbed an arm of each of his sons and yanked them apart. "Haven't I told you about fighting in the house?"

Jenny's hands flew to her hips. "Danny started it."

Danny made a face at Jenny and stuck out his tongue. "Tattletale."

"Let the sheriff handle this, Jenny."

"Yes, ma'am."

Josh released his grip on the boys and dusted his hands as if dismissing the problem. "Sorry if they woke you, Chrysie. I had to leave them alone for a minute to take a phone call."

Alarm kicked in. Had he changed his mind and been talking to someone in Houston about her? She studied his expression but saw nothing to indicate he'd turned on her.

"Can I get you some breakfast?" he asked. "So far the choices are cereal or toast and jelly."

She glanced at the table. The blue checkered table-cloth was decorated with a large orange stain. One cereal bowl was overturned, as was a box of something that looked like chocolate puffs being passed off as breakfast food.

"Guess it doesn't look too appetizing," Josh said, no doubt reading her expression. "We had a few problems."

She poured herself a cup of coffee, then sat down at the end of the table while Josh started clearing the mess. He might be a terrific rancher and sheriff, but his parenting skills were sadly lacking. If she stayed around long enough, she'd do something about that. The boys needed firm but loving guidance.

Jenny climbed back into a kitchen chair. "I told Sheriff Josh that you didn't let us eat that kind of cereal."

"It won't hurt you to have it once, and it was nice of the sheriff to fix breakfast for you. I hope you remembered to thank him."

"Well, I couldn't thank him yet 'cause I haven't had breakfast. I'm waiting on toast and grape jelly."

Mandy walked to stand beside Chrysie. "Can we go home now?"

Chrysie took another sip of the coffee. Her mind was clearer this morning, but she still hadn't come up with any suitable way to explain that they would be living here in this tiny cabin with people they barely knew. She'd put the girls through so much in their young lives, dragging them from place to place, afraid to make close friends, afraid to let them out of her sight. She knew that overbearing parenting could be as harmful as neglect, but given the circumstances, she hadn't had much choice.

She lifted Mandy to her lap and kissed her chubby cheek. "We're going to be staying with the McCains for a while," she said.

"Why?"

Chrysie looked to Josh, wondering if he'd given his boys an answer to that question. He obviously read her raised eyebrows as a request for help. He dropped to his knees so he was eye level with Mandy. "Your house had a big leak in the roof and all that snow is melting and pouring in. If you were there, you'd have to walk around with your raincoat on."

"That would be funny."

"Right on, but your toys and books would get all wet, and that would be bad, so you'd better stay with us."

The answer seemed to satisfy Mandy, at least for now. Chrysie mouthed her thanks over Mandy's head.

So here she was in league with the sheriff. It was a strange bonding, one fraught with frightening possibilities. He could at any moment decide she was guilty or that the risk of harboring her was too great.

One call to the Houston Police Department and she could be on her way to jail. For all she knew, he'd made the call already and was only waiting for the authorities to pick her up.

Yet sitting here at his kitchen table, dressed in her polka-dot jammies, her hair disheveled from sleep, she felt more awkward than uneasy—awkward and much too keenly aware of the sexy, charismatic sheriff hovering over her.

"I make a mean scrambled egg," Josh said.

"Good, I was afraid I'd have to settle for sugar-coated chocolate lumps."

"No, the gourmet stuff is just for the kids."

Mandy climbed down from her lap and went running to the den, where the boys were howling in laughter over whatever was happening on Saturday-morning cartoons. Jenny wolfed down her toast so she could join them, as well.

Which left Chrysie alone with Josh. When the eggs were ready, he set them on the table along with four slices of toasted and buttered bread and joined her for breakfast.

"Guess we should talk strategy," he said.

"Strategy as in how six people are going to live in a house with one bathroom and two bedrooms?"

"No, I've got that worked out."

"Really?"

"Sure. We sleep in shifts. You and the girls get the

first half of the night. The boys and I will take the second half. And we'll only bathe every other day."

She choked, and the bite of egg she was chewing went down the wrong path. Josh jumped up and slapped her on the back a few times, knocking the egg and her tonsils loose.

"I was joking," he said. "You can have my bed and the girls can take the bunk beds. I'll get some sleeping bags for the boys and we'll camp out on the den floor. It'll be fun."

"You don't have to do this."

"Do you have a better suggestion?"

"You can forget you ever saw me and the girls, and I can just disappear from your life?"

"I like my option better."

She took another bite of egg. She chewed slowly, reassessing the situation, amazed that she could be eating at all when her whole life had taken a serious turn for the worse over the past twenty-four hours.

"We need to set priorities," Josh said. "I think the first order of business should be discovering the identity of the men who killed your husband."

"I don't know how you'd do that. I'd never seen them before that night."

"They likely have a police record. Do you think you can identify them from a mug shot?"

"I'm sure I could. I've seen those faces in a hundred nightmares. But if you call the Houston police and ask for that information, they'll suspect something."

"Right, which is why I won't call them. But I have friends in high places. Actually, I have friends in low places, too, both of which could be helpful."

Apprehension started churning again, and Chrysie pushed her plate away, her appetite totally vanished. Even the thought of seeing the two men's mug shots made her nauseous.

I'll see what I can dig up," Josh said, "but it would help if we knew the motive for the murders."

"I'm certain it was just a robbery gone bad. Jonathan probably woke up while they were burglarizing the house, and the crooks killed him."

"If that's the case, why did they hang around and wait for you to return?"

"I don't know they waited. I just happened in on them right after they'd killed him."

"Did your husband keep a gun in the house?"

"Yes, but he'd never used it."

"Had anyone made threats on his life?"

"No. Everyone liked Jonathan."

"A popular lawyer. That's sort of an oxymoron, isn't it?"

"Well, I'm sure he had enemies in the business sense but never anything personal."

Josh's cell phone rang. He excused himself and walked outside to take the call, out of her hearing range. That made her nervous, too. If this was about her, then she should be able to hear the conversation. And if it wasn't about her, there was still no need for secrecy. She took the dishes to the sink and rinsed them. Josh returned before she was finished.

"You are not to do dishes or housework today. Doctor's orders."

"I feel fine." That was a blatant lie, but she was pretty sure it was the situation and not the bump to her head yesterday that was causing the nagging pain at the base of her skull.

"Nonetheless, you're supposed to get bed rest."

"Okay, right after I shower."

"I have to be out for a while this afternoon."

"You're leaving?"

"For a couple of hours. I have to take care of some business, but I'll take the boys with me so you can have some quiet. If you want, I can take the girls, too."

"No. They'll be fine. They play quietly." Her mind jumped into gear. A couple of hours would be plenty of time for her to get out of town, but she'd need a car. Perhaps she could call Evelyn and borrow one of the pickup trucks Buck used on the ranch.

Josh took another call. Chrysie headed for the shower, her mind running with ideas for escape. It wasn't that she didn't appreciate Josh's help, but he thought he could keep her safe while he conducted his investigation. But he was a small-town sheriff. What did he know of men who were evil through and through?

"MAC BUCKLEY PUT the jar to his lips and shook out a mouthful of peanuts. A few rolled down his bare stomach, across his briefs and onto the worn leather sofa. This was his favorite night for watching TV. There was one crime show after another, all ones where the good guys won in the end.

Americans were so gullible. They actually believed that cops and forensics experts were the only ones who had access to all that information. Hell, he knew as much as any of them.

The phone rang. The calling number came up on his TV screen. There was no name, but the number had a Houston area code. Could be business.

"Hello."

"Hello, Mac."

Definitely business. "What's up?"

"Cassandra Harwell. I think she may have been spotted in Montana, possibly in or near a town called Aohkii."

"Well, it's about time."

"I want you and Sean to make a trip up there and check things out. The sheriff who called to get information on Cassandra is Josh McCain."

"I'll be on the first plane out of town. Any special instructions?"

"Kill her and leave no witnesses. And don't do anything that would connect the killing to Texas or the Harwell murder case."

"You got it."

He broke the connection and went back to the TV show and the peanuts, but the excitement was already building. He'd wanted to kill the tight-ass doctor in the first place, but the rules had been different then.

He liked the new rules better. Dead people never talked.

Chapter Six

The plans for escape that Chrysie had made in the shower fell apart the second she walked back into the kitchen and ran into a man with a bowling ball for a gut that pushed his belt down to near no-man's-land.

He smiled when she walked into the room. His teeth were tobacco-brown, but he had nice eyes that crinkled at the edges and sparkled as if he were watching fireworks. And now he was one more person who knew who she was or at least that she was in the sheriff's unofficial custody.

Josh made the introductions, then pulled her aside while Cougar walked out the back door to spit a stream of brown gunk over the porch rail and into the snow.

"Are you sure you're feeling all right?" Josh asked.

"Are you going to ask that every five minutes?"

"I'm not used to playing nurse."

"Obviously. Nurses wait until you drop off to sleep so they can wake you before asking that."

"I'll try to remember that. In the meantime, Cougar is a good guy, dependable and great with kids. He can watch the girls while you rest."

"I'm sure he has better things to do on a Saturday afternoon. And isn't it unethical for you to use a deputy to watch an unofficial prisoner?"

"Might be if I were paying him with county money. I told him I had a hot woman that needed looking after, and he volunteered his services."

"Why don't you just take out an ad in the community newspaper and tell everyone who I am and why I'm here?"

"Take it easy. I didn't tell him the whole story."

"So is he a deputy or not?"

"He's only part-time now, just helps when I need him, but he was the sheriff here for years up until he stepped on some criminal's inalienable rights a few years back. He was cleared at the hearing, but by then he'd told them what they could do with the sheriff position. He'd been threatening to retire for years anyway."

"Which rights did he step on?"

"He broke a couple of the guy's ribs."

"That's supposed to make me feel better about this?"

"The guy had it coming. He was a no-good drug dealer who was using his own sons to deliver the goods to other teenagers. Besides, the other guy took the first swing."

"Now you sound like Davy and Danny. Exactly what did you tell Cougar about me?"

"That you need my protective services."

"That's it?"

"And that he was not to let you leave the house for any reason unless he was with you."

"That should be just enough information to whet his appetite and send him to the same missing-persons Web site you visited."

"Why would he? You'll have him so charmed by the time I get back he'll be ready to break a few hips for you."

"Sure, I'm a real femme fatale."

"You're not half-bad—for a fugitive."

He smiled and she felt flushed. It was unthinkable that she could respond to him in this situation, but there wasn't a lot she could do about it except try to keep her distance—while they shared a tiny cabin and she slept in his bed.

Cougar stepped back inside, closing the storm door behind him with a rattling bang. He nodded in her direction but walked though the kitchen and into the den, where the boys were tossing a foam football around and, judging from the noise, performing spectacular athletic jumps from falling furniture. Her girls were back in the boys' bedroom playing with their dolls.

Josh's gaze lifted and locked with hers. "I hope to be back in a couple of hours, three at the most. I programmed my cell number into your phone while you were showering. Call me if you need anything."

"I need a car."

He ignored her. "The first order of business is rest, but if you need something to occupy your mind, I'd like you to start making a list of everything you know about your late husband's hobbies and business dealings. List everything that pops into your mind, even the things that don't seem important. Put a star by anything that changed over the last few weeks and months before his murder."

"I've had three years to think about this, Josh. I haven't come up with a single reason why someone other than burglars caught red-handed would kill Jonathan. The answers aren't going to just all of a sudden pop out of my memory bank because I make a list."

"Just give it a try. We'll talk later."

The football came flying into the kitchen. Josh put up a hand, caught it and tossed it back into the den without hesitating on a single syllable. She hoped his reflexes were as good when it came to intercepting killers. He might need the skill before this was over.

She prayed it didn't come to that, but the fear was welling inside her again. She doubted even Josh was a match for those monsters. She was almost positive Cougar wasn't.

CHRYSIE AND COUGAR made small talk, mostly about the weather and the rising price of gasoline. She knew it was best to keep him at a distance so that he didn't feel free to ask any personal questions, but her curiosity about Josh had grown proportionately with her traitorous attraction.

She picked up the cushions that had been scattered about the room during the boys' rambunctious game of indoor football and placed them on the couch. "Have you known Josh a long time?" she asked.

"Ever since he moved to Montana. That's been about seven years now."

Seven years ago. That would be before the boys were born but possibly after they were conceived— or maybe not.

Cougar rubbed his whiskered chin. "Most guys grow wilder once they move to Montana. Josh has actually tamed a bit."

"Tamed? In what way?"

"He was a loner with an attitude. Most folks like that get their attitude adjusted pretty quickly up here, but Josh could hold his own with anybody."

"Odd that a guy like that would end up as sheriff."

"It's 'cause he ran deeper than what he wanted you to believe. Folks liked him in spite of himself, and he was a hard worker. Buck Miller says he was the first one on the job in the morning and the last one in the bunkhouse at night. Likable, not afraid to take on anything or anybody and not afraid of hard work. He was a natural to replace me. 'Course, he didn't have two sons to raise back then. Didn't even go by the name of Josh McCain."

"What name did he go by?"

"Josh Morgan."

"Why did he use an alias?"

"I don't know. I figure he had his reasons. We don't mess much with people's private lives up here. You either cut it or you don't."

Apparently Josh had cut it. But a man didn't change his last name unless he had a purpose for doing so. Had his own past been suspect? Was that why he'd believed her story or at least decided to investigate further before turning her over to the Houston police?

"Josh is a good guy, but don't push him, Chrysie. A man like Josh don't like to be pushed and he sure won't take being lied to." Cougar gave the warning, then picked up the remote and powered on the TV.

Chrysie took that as a signal that he was through talking. She stepped into the narrow hallway to go and check on the girls. The two of them played well together despite the age difference—as long as Jenny didn't get too bossy. Chrysie paused when she was near enough to hear their conversation clearly.

"I hope Santa Claus knows we had a flood at our

house," Mandy said. "I don't want my presents to get all wet."

"It wasn't a flood," Jenny corrected. "It was a leak. That's different. And I hope I get a puppy."

Jenny had begged for a puppy ever since they'd left Houston. It broke Chrysie's heart that she couldn't get her one, but pets didn't fit in a nomadic lifestyle or in the small apartments they'd lived in before now.

The Miller cabin would have been the perfect spot for a dog. The animal would have acres to explore, and Jenny could have run with him, through the grass, along the creeks and up and down the mountain paths.

Chrysie leaned against the wall, suddenly weak and more than a little heartsick. It wasn't going to happen, not for Jenny and not for Mandy.

"I'd rather have a daddy than a puppy," Mandy said. "A daddy can give you shoulder rides, just like Sheriff Josh does. And he can pick up really big Christmas trees and stuff. And get your car started when Mommy can't."

Chrysie swallowed hard. A puppy was out of the question. Josh McCain as Mandy's daddy was about as likely as…as Santa actually arriving in a sleigh pulled by flying deer with glowing noses.

"I don't think Santa brings daddies," Jenny said. "You better just ask for a puppy. We might get lucky."

Christmas was two weeks away. That would give Josh plenty of time to check out her story and make his decision. If he let Chrysie go without arresting her, she might just see that her girls got that puppy and make room for it in the crowded car when it was time to move on.

If he didn't believe her, then she might be spending Christmas in jail, and her daughters could be stuck in an orphanage with total strangers who had no idea how special they were.

They wouldn't know that Jenny liked her bath lukewarm and that she was afraid of loud thunder. They wouldn't know Mandy had nightmares sometimes and that the only thing that calmed her was a story or that she loved chocolate sprinkles on top of her ice cream.

The girls had gone back to their dolls now, and Jenny was telling hers she would take her for a walk in her stroller but that she better not cry and scare the cows. Chrysie tiptoed by the bedroom unnoticed, unwilling for the girls to see her tears.

This was no time for weakness. Yet when she reached the room at the end of the hall and the unmade bed she'd slept in last night, she fell to the crumpled sheets and sobbed herself to sleep.

JOSH HAD GOTTEN ONLY one official call that day: a stranger in a red pickup truck had driven away from the local service station without paying for his gas.

Fortunately the forgetful driver had returned to pay his bill even before Josh had hung up from the complaint call.

Josh stretched, closed his eyes for a second, then pushed back from the computer. He'd just completed the frustrating task of scrutinizing a long list of violent thefts in Houston, Texas, over the last three years. None of them had occurred in the same area as the Harwell murder.

The boys were suspiciously quiet, so he walked to the door and peeked into the outer office where they had been playing. Davy had fallen asleep in the old worn chair under the window. Danny was watching an animated movie on Josh's laptop.

"Can we go now?" Danny said without looking up from the screen. "I'm tired of this old office."

"Yeah, just give me a minute to shut down the computer and make a few notes."

His phone rang before he finished. It was Clayton Green, one of his buddies from his college days, who was currently an FBI agent in San Antonio. "What did you get?" Josh asked, forgoing the routine hello.

"A couple of things. One, a lawyer named Marv Evinu had been given the power of attorney in case either Jonathan Harwell or his wife Cassandra weren't around to handle their estate. He's handled their finances and kept up their house payments and property taxes on their home."

"So the house is still in Mrs. Harwell's name?"

"Exactly. I haven't been able to get my hands on the crime-scene report yet, but I did get one of the guys in the crime lab down there to fax me the firearms and ballistics report."

"What did you find?"

"That it's very unlikely that Cassandra Harwell is as innocent as she claims."

CHRYSIE STARED at the top of the stairs, livid and so terrified that her lungs burned with each gasp for air. "Put her down. Put my baby down."

The monster laughed and held Mandy farther over the banister, shaking her tiny body so that her little legs seemed to be dancing.

Heart pounding, Chrysie started to race up the staircase. But the wooden steps started revolving, the flights going in random directions so that every step took her farther and farther away from Mandy and the brute who held her. Chrysie's hands were numb, frozen to a block of ice that was clasped in her right hand. Only it wasn't ice. It was a pistol, a shiny silver pistol.

She held it up and aimed it, but the steps started revolving again, this time spinning wildly. She fell and the gun went off. There was a huge thud and blood, so much blood, all over the stairs—and the bed. All over Jonathan.

Chrysie jerked awake. Her T-shirt was wet from the cold sweat that pooled between her breasts. She'd had some version of the nightmare hundreds of time before. It was never exactly the same except for the ending. Jonathan was always lying in a pool of blood, and she could never reach Mandy.

She knew enough about dreams to understand that the nightmares were a manifestation of the frustration and fear she lived with every day. Nothing she did could save Jonathan. And she could never guarantee that the monster wouldn't get his hands on Mandy again.

Chrysie went to the bathroom, splashed her face with cold water and ran her fingers through her short hair. During the first few months after the murder, any glance into a mirror had produced a shock, the bizarre feeling that a stranger had crawled inside her and taken over her body.

The changes in appearance were even more dramatic now that she'd gained a few pounds and her skin was bronzed from the sun. But the biggest differences were on the inside. Then, much of her identity had been tied to her career as a psychologist and her position as Jonathan's wife. Now she was only Chrysie Atwater, mother.

She glanced at her watch. She'd slept almost two hours. Apprehension sent her scurrying down the hall in search of the girls. She was not used to having them out of her sight that long unless they were at preschool or asleep. She found them in the living room playing with some toy dinosaurs that evidently belonged to the boys. Cougar was watching a college football game on the television.

Mandy jumped up and ran to her. "We were quiet so you could sleep and get well fast."

"Yes you were, and I appreciate that." Chrysie reached down, picked her up and gave her a big hug before setting her back to the floor.

"This is a Tyrannosaurus rex," Jenny said, holding the plastic replica up so that Chrysie could get a better look. "He's carnivorous. That means he eats meat, like other dinosaurs. That's what Mr. Cougar said. But tyrannosaurs didn't eat people. He lived so long ago there weren't any people."

"Sounds as if you've learned a lot about dinosaurs while I slept."

"I tried to keep 'em busy," Cougar said. "Josh called a few minutes ago. He's on his way home, should be here in ten minutes or so, said he was bringing pizza."

Jenny and Mandy clapped their hands in unison. Chrysie went to the kitchen for a glass of water and to rummage drawers for a pad and pencil to start her list of things she knew about Jonathan. She had no idea where to start unless she began with the lie that had permeated their whole marriage.

She had never loved Jonathan Harwell.

Chapter Seven

It was midafternoon before Josh managed a few minutes alone with Chrysie, and even then they weren't really alone. The kids were running and playing ahead of them while they walked in the snow. Chrysie had said she needed some fresh air. He understood that feeling all too well. He'd felt cooped up all his life, never feeling he could breathe free until he'd arrived in Montana.

That first morning on Buck Miller's ranch, when he'd smelled the scent of hay, felt the sun hot on his back even while the air was brisk, seen green as far as he could see, he'd known he was home.

And now he had it all. His own ranch. The opportunity to work in law enforcement—even though it wasn't the type of investigative work he'd envisioned when he'd caught his first Dirty Harry movie on late-night TV. He even had two adorable sons. He adjusted his Stetson, pulling the brim down to shade his eyes from the sun. Yep, he had it all.

So why was he putting it on the line for a woman he barely knew? That had been the question his FBI buddy had posed on the phone once he'd realized what Josh was up to. Josh could call this protective custody until his own cows came home, but the Houston police would see it as aiding and abetting, especially with the evidence they had against Chrysie.

She slipped, and he put out a hand to steady her. Still she fell against him for a moment before regaining her balance. His chest tightened and an unwanted arousal stirred between his legs.

What was there about her that got to him like this? He'd been with lots of women, some prettier than Chrysie. Some sexier. Some with better bodies. Not that she was lacking in any of those departments.

He'd like to blame it on the fact that she was in serious jeopardy, but even that didn't tell it all. There was just some kind of weird chemistry between them. He'd felt it the first night at the civic center. And right now he felt it way down in his gut—and a couple of very sensitive places in between.

This was getting him nowhere. "Did you make the list about Jonathan?" he asked, trying to get his mind and libido back on track.

"I wrote down a few things." She pulled a piece

of paper from the back pocket of her jeans, unfolded it and handed it to him.

"You say here he was determined to become a wealthy and powerful man. Was that always the case?"

"Pretty much. His father was an alcoholic and never kept a job for more than a few months at a time. Jonathan had quit school in the tenth grade to help support his family."

"Yet he ended up with a law degree," Josh said, thinking out loud as much as making conversation.

"He earned his graduate equivalency degree at night school, then worked afternoons and nights to put himself through university."

"Did you notice anything different about his moods or work habits in the days and weeks just prior to his murder?"

"I didn't see much of him."

"Because of the affair with his secretary?"

"No. We'd drifted apart months before that. Looking back, I guess I shouldn't have been surprised by the affair, except that…" Her voice trailed off.

"I'm in this neck-deep, Chrysie. Don't hold back on me."

"We'd been having marital problems since before I got pregnant with Mandy. I'd mentioned a separation, but Jonathan was dead set against it. He kept saying we could make the marriage work. He'd even agreed to marriage counseling. We had already made an appointment for the week after he was murdered."

"Then I can see why the affair caught you off guard. How did he react when you questioned him about the affair?"

"He denied it, said I was imagining things, that it was just my postpartum depression talking."

A red flag shot up, waving like crazy in Josh's head. "You never mentioned being depressed."

"Because I wasn't. I loved being a mother."

"What about your career? Were you happy with that?"

"Very, though I had cut back on my hours during my pregnancy with Mandy and hadn't resumed a full schedule yet. She was only two months old."

A marriage going sour. A husband accused of having an affair. A wife who might or might not have been suffering from postpartum depression. And the cops in Houston no doubt knew all of this.

The air was shattered by a loud squeal. Josh and Chrysie took off running. They found Jenny on the ground, her face and hair frosted with snow.

"I was making snow angels, and Danny and Davy hit me in the face with snowballs." Her words were more like sputters between sobs.

Josh looked around. There was no sign of the boys. He called and then whistled loudly. They walked up slowly, mittened hands stuck in their pockets and looking like innocent angels who'd been called back to earth for unjustified punishment.

"We were just playing attack," Danny said. "Davy hits me with snowballs all the time. They don't hurt."

"I wasn't playing attack," Jenny said. "And they smashed them in my face."

"Okay, boys. You'll have to be punished."

The boys stared at him as if he'd just ordered them to be shot at daybreak or at least tortured and made to shovel snow. He felt like a cad, but then, Jenny had been on the ground and kind of defenseless when they'd ganged up on her.

"She's just a big crybaby," Danny said. "And this is our house anyway. Who wants her here?"

Chrysie reached out and took both boys by their arms. "Look at me."

They hesitated but finally turned their faces toward her.

"Throwing snowballs is one thing," she said in a voice that sounded as authoritative as God might have used issuing the Ten Commandments. "Smashing them in someone's face when they're not playing attack is unacceptable behavior. I think a ten-minute time-out in your room with no TV or toys while you think about what you've done is appropriate punishment."

"Yes, ma'am," Danny said.

"And you owe Jenny a genuine apology."

Danny looked back to his boots and kicked at the snow. "I'm sorry, Jenny."

"Me, too," Davy said. "I won't smash you again unless you're playing attack."

Josh stood there in awe of Chrysie's performance and dumbfounded by his sons' obedient responses. She was good, damn good. No wonder people had paid her big bucks to work with their troubled children.

They took a shortcut back to the house, but not short enough that the boys retained their subdued moods. They were running ahead, pummeling each other with snowballs until they ended up on the ground in a mass of tangled arms and legs, laughing while they scuffled and rolled about in the snow.

Jenny walked between her mother and Josh, ending any chance of his asking Chrysie about the information he'd gotten from his FBI friend. Mandy dawdled and lagged behind, until she ran up and grabbed Josh's hand.

"I'm tired," she said. "Can I ride on your shoulders?"

Josh picked her up and swung her into place, amazed again at how light she was. The boys had been only a little older than she was now when he'd seen them for the very first time.

They'd been half-afraid of him at first. But then, they'd already lived through hell. The police had gotten the details surrounding their mother's death all wrong.

But were they wrong about Chrysie or was he letting sentiments from his own past and his almost overpowering attraction for her affect his judgment?

"Oooh, look!" Mandy called, kicking so enthusiastically he had to grab her feet to keep her from bouncing off his shoulders.

Josh looked, but all he saw was a tall spruce that stretched a couple of feet over his head.

"It's a Christmas tree," Mandy said. "Can we get it, please?"

"It's much too tall," Chrysie said.

"I don't know about that," Josh said. "It looks like a pretty perfect Christmas tree to me."

"Yes," Mandy agreed. "Perfect."

"I don't know where you'd put it," Chrysie said. "There's no place for everyone to sleep as it is."

True, but then, he figured they all needed a little Christmas about now. And if a little was good, then a lot should be better. "We can put it in the middle of the den and the boys and I can put our sleeping bags beneath it. It will be like camping outdoors, except we'll be warm."

"There's no room, Josh."

She was using that authoritative voice that had scared the boys into instant submission. But, hell, he was the sheriff. "We'll come back for it tomorrow," he announced.

He could give Mandy this, but it wasn't nearly

enough. Someone had to step in and give her, Jenny and Chrysie back their lives. It might as well be him, unless—

Unless he found out Chrysie was guilty of murder. And then it would be his duty to destroy Mandy's and Jenny's lives.

So, yeah, even if it took up every square foot of the room and he had to sleep in the bathtub, Mandy could have her tree.

THE HOUSE WAS QUIET except for the boys' breathing. Josh lay very still, listening to the soft, rhythmic sound. When they'd first come to live with him, he'd gotten up several times a night to walk to the door of their room and listen to that sound. It had seemed a miracle then that he could have fathered two such marvelous sons.

He still marveled, but he took them for granted now. At least he had until Chrysie had dropped into his life. It was impossible to see the fear in her eyes when she talked of the men who'd threatened her children without imagining how he'd feel if someone wanted to hurt Davy or Danny.

But pairing her story with what he'd learned today was like trying to round up cattle with no markings or means of identification. There was no place to start, no way to a solution.

He tiptoed to the bathroom, took a hot shower

and slipped into a pair of clean jeans, only half zipping them and not bothering with the button at all since he was only going to the kitchen for a glass of cold milk before he climbed into his sleeping bag.

But when he stepped out of the bathroom, he heard soft footfalls coming from the back of the house. He'd thought Chrysie was asleep, but apparently she was still awake and walking around in the bedroom—*his* bedroom. He swallowed hard as his pulse jumped a notch and his jeans tightened around his groin.

You'd think a murder case and all the complications that accompanied this one would put a damper on sexual cravings. But then, he knew that wasn't the case. That's the reason bodyguards fell for the people they were protecting and cops got taken in by beautiful suspects. Tension begat tension. An attraction that might quietly simmer along under normal conditions escalated to blazing in the face of danger.

He'd have to keep his blaze in the furnace a while longer, but he did need to talk to Chrysie. He knocked softly on the closed bedroom door.

She opened it a crack.

"Can I come in? Just to talk?" he added before she got the wrong idea.

She eased the door open. She wasn't in the flannel jammies she'd been in that morning but a pair of soft yellow ones made of some kind of silky material that clung just enough that he could see the outline of her breasts beneath the barely exposed cleavage.

He averted his gaze before his needs got out of hand. "Do you feel like talking?"

"Yes, but I don't know what else I can tell you. My husband was murdered in his bed. That's all I know."

She was definitely not leveling with him. "I'm just trying to get a handle on everything."

"Then ask away."

He walked across the room and leaned his backside against his pine dresser. "How did you find out your husband was having an affair with his secretary?"

"I had gone into my office for a few hours the way I did every morning. When I got home, the babysitter handed me a brown envelope that she said had been dropped off by courier."

"Which courier?"

"There were no markings on it to show which service had made the delivery. At any rate, I opened it, and it was a photograph of Jonathan and Vanessa locked in a disgusting embrace. The top buttons on her blouse were undone and he was cupping her buttocks in his hands."

"Pretty coincidental to find that out on the same day your husband was murdered."

She bristled, and her eyes fired as if backlit by a

torch. "I don't know why I thought you'd believe me when none of the Houston police did."

"I didn't say I don't believe you."

"You said it. You just didn't use those exact words."

"What did the cops say when you told them about the photo?"

"I didn't tell them. They found it when they were investigating the crime scene. I'd stupidly left it behind when I'd slammed out of the house that night, and Jonathan had tossed it on the floor near the bed."

Chrysie dropped to the edge of the bed. Josh started to sit down beside her but thought better of it. He walked to the chair in front of the window and perched on its upholstered arm.

"So you hadn't told the police what you and Jonathan had argued about?"

"Not originally. I just told them we were having marital problems and things had come to a head that night. It wasn't a total lie."

But it was a lie. "You said you think Jonathan was killed in a foiled burglary attempt. What did they steal?"

"Nothing. But they would have if Jonathan hadn't woken up and I hadn't come in on them."

"Okay, let's see if I have this straight. Two men killed your husband and threatened to kill the girls if you said you'd seen them. They were brazen and evil, but they just walked away with nothing and didn't actually harm you?"

"I know it sounds bizarre, but that's what happened."

"Did the police question you about the gun that was used in the murder?"

"How did you find out about the gun?"

"The question is, why didn't you tell me that the police found the gun in the bushes in back of your house with your prints all over it?"

Chrysie started to shake. "I had the gun, Josh. I picked it up and aimed it at the monster who was holding Mandy over the railing. I wanted to kill him. I did. But if I had, he would have dropped her."

"When did you throw it in the bushes, Chrysie? Before you called the police? Or did you hide it and dispose of it later?"

"I didn't dispose of the gun. I threw it down when the second guy ordered me to and I never saw it again. I know how this sounds, but I never hid the gun. And the police never mentioned to me that they'd found it."

She turned to him. Her eyes were wide, frightened. Her lips quivered. "You think I killed Jonathan, don't you?"

No. Heaven help him if he was wrong, but he believed her. He ached to take her in his arms and kiss away her fears. He should go before he did anything that stupid.

Only he couldn't. He sat down on the bed beside her and wrapped his arm around her trembling shoulders. She rested against him, as soft as a pillow of clover.

And then his lips were on hers, and any vestiges of sane thoughts were stripped from his mind.

He knew he was making a monumental mistake. But still he didn't pull away.

CHRYSIE TREMBLED AS Josh's lips claimed hers. The passion surging through her was almost as frightening as the fear, the sweet, salty taste of Josh's mouth foreign and forbidden. It was the wrong time, the wrong place, the wrong man. But the kiss deepened, and she couldn't fight the thrill of Josh McCain along with everything else she had to battle.

Moments or breathtaking minutes later, Josh jerked away. His rejection hurt—until she heard the sounds. First a creak, then footfalls in the hall, so soft they were almost indistinguishable. She struggled for breath and composure as her youngest daughter pushed through the door.

"I had a bad dream." Mandy padded across the room, but instead of coming to Chrysie for comfort, she climbed into Josh's lap. He gave her a hug. It was all so innocent and natural, yet Chrysie felt as if the air had been sucked from her lungs.

For three years Chrysie had kept her daughters

safe by erecting barriers that no one could break through. Now Chrysie was letting Josh's nearness and a sexual attraction with no basis in reality weaken her defenses at the time she needed her survival skills and instincts at their sharpest.

Josh pushed loose locks of Mandy's hair from a cheek that still held the crease marks from her bed linens. "You don't need to worry about bad dreams," he said. "I'm the sheriff. Nobody can hurt you when you're sleeping in the sheriff's house."

"Not even monsters?"

"Nightmare monsters are my specialty."

Mandy smiled and gave him another hug. A promise from Josh was all she needed to make her feel safe again. But Mandy was totally unaware that the sheriff who promised protection so easily could turn on them at any second.

One phone call and he could have Chrysie on her way to jail, leaving Mandy and Jenny all alone and giving the real monsters free rein to exact revenge in any way they saw fit.

"I'll take you back to bed and lie down with you a while," Chrysie said, standing and reaching for her daughter. Mandy slid into her arms and wrapped her legs around Chrysie's waist as they walked the narrow hallway.

Josh followed close behind. He trailed a finger down Chrysie's arm when she reached the door to the bedroom the girls had taken over. "I didn't mean to upset you."

"You didn't." She couldn't keep the edge from her voice, but she couldn't lay the blame for the kiss solely on him.

Josh lingered. "If you need me, you know where I am."

She knew. Guarding the door and so clued in to the least sound that he'd heard Mandy's footsteps in the hall long before she had. He'd definitely know if Chrysie tried to escape with the children during the night.

"Good night, Mandy," he whispered. "And sweet dreams—no nightmares allowed."

"Okay."

Chrysie laid her daughter on the bottom bunk bed and tucked her under the covers before stretching to her tiptoes to check on Jenny. She was sleeping soundly, a stuffed alligator that belonged to one of the boys clasped tightly to her chest.

Moonlight filtered through the curtained windows in silver planes and angles, giving the pine furniture a magical glow. A rustic cabin, a simple lifestyle, but Josh McCain was anything but a simple man. He'd used an alias when he'd first come to Montana. For all she knew, his past could be as complicated and convoluted as hers. She'd love to know, but she didn't dare ask. Shared secrets would only strengthen the weird bonds that already held them.

Chrysie dropped to the one chair in the room, an antique rocker that sat just beneath the window. It creaked softly as she settled into the cushions and rested her head against the high back. She closed her eyes, but opened them again when thoughts of Josh's kiss slipped into her mind.

She forced her mind to concentrate on the things Josh had brought up tonight. The gun with her prints on it. The fact that the men she was so certain were thieves hadn't really taken anything. The coincidence of receiving the photograph of Jonathan and Vanessa less than twenty-four hours before Jonathan was killed.

And there in the moonlight of a frigid Montana night, a new possibility took root in her mind: the murder may have been planned and she might have been set up to take the rap.

Her first impulse was to tiptoe into the den, where Josh had bedded down in his new sleeping bag, and tell him her revelation. But once she thought about it, she knew he was too good a sheriff not to have put it together the same way she had.

So why hadn't he just come right out and said it? Had he just been playing her, trying to read her re-actions to the information he'd gathered?

She wouldn't confront him tonight. Her lips were still sweetly swollen, her body still smoldering from the burst of unfamiliar passion. She couldn't risk so much as a touch between them.

Only how would she avoid that when they ate at the same table, shared the same shower, breathed the same air? The answer lay in the two girls sleeping near her in unfamiliar bunk beds.

She'd do whatever it took to keep them safe.

Chapter Eight

Breakfast for six was the expected madhouse, though so far there had been no spills or major brawls. Danny and Mandy had, however, managed to get syrup from their pancakes all over the fronts of their pajama tops. Davy was currently bobbing for marshmallows in his hot chocolate, forming quite an impressive moustache.

And Jenny was talking a mile a minute, hoping no one would notice that she'd broken her pancake in little pieces and shoved them all to the middle of her plate so that it looked as if she'd eaten a lot more than she actually had. If Chrysie had Jenny's appetite, it would eliminate a lot of early morning ab crunches.

"Glad I stopped at the grocer's yesterday and restocked the cupboards and fridge," Josh said. "Breakfasts like that don't come along every day."

"Definitely not if I'm the cook," Chrysie said. "It's oatmeal and toast the rest of the week."

"Mommy makes great French toast," Jenny said.

The boys licked their lips and made yummy sounds. Mandy followed suit. She was starting to mimic everything the boys did, and that could turn into a major problem. Chrysie was making an effort to correct the boys' lack of table manners today. However, she knew deep down her attempt was halfhearted due to the short time she expected to be here.

Josh started to gather the empty plates. "Tell me you can make grits, and I'll…" He let the end of the sentence trail off.

The easy mood vanished, replaced by heavy-duty tension. The standard finish for the line was "and I'll marry you." Yesterday, he could have blurted that right out. It was last night's kiss that made it awkward now. That and the fact that they'd been sitting at the table laughing and talking like a real family and not one bound by bad luck and Josh's off-kilter sense of justice.

Danny bumped elbows with Davy, then jumped down from the table and took off running, knowing his twin brother would follow.

Josh caught him before he got to the door, yanking him to a screeching halt. "No playing until you get out of those sticky pajamas and wash every bit of syrup from your face and hands."

"I wiped them on the napkin."

"Not good enough."

"You wouldn't make us be so clean if Chrysie wasn't here."

"I wouldn't need to. We wouldn't have had pancakes and syrup. Now hop to it. Get dressed. You, too, Davy. When everyone's ready, I have a surprise."

"Is the surprise for us, too?" Jenny asked.

"Absolutely. I wouldn't leave out the three prettiest ladies in the county."

"What is this surprise?" Chrysie asked, annoyed that he'd announce they were doing anything without consulting her first.

"We're going to cut down a Christmas tree."

Mandy jumped down from her chair and ran to Josh. "My Christmas tree?"

"You betcha. The finest Christmas tree I've ever seen."

Danny gave a loud whoop. "Can we take the four-wheeler?"

"We'd never all fit. Besides, I'm doing some work on it."

There was a chorus of complaints from Mandy and the boys, though Chrysie was certain Mandy had no idea what a four-wheeler was.

"We're taking the sleigh," Josh announced.

Mandy's eyes grew wide. She tugged on Josh's sleeve with her sticky fingers. "A real sleigh, like Santa has?"

"Nicer than Santa's. We'll have to use horses to

pull it, though. The reindeer are all up at the North Pole getting ready for their big night."

"I rode a horse once," Jenny said.

"So what?" Danny taunted. "Me and Davy ride horses all the time."

"And Jenny can start riding them all the time, too, if she wants," Josh said. "But right now we're going on a sleigh ride."

The four-wheeler forgotten, the youngsters dashed from the kitchen, their laughter echoing down the hallway. The sound curled around Chrysie's heart, in spite of the growing apprehension. She took a deep breath, determined to push the fear behind her for at least the duration of the sleigh ride—or at least to subdue it enough she wouldn't ruin the excitement for everyone else.

She gathered parkas, hats and boots and helped the kids into the bulky paraphernalia, even though none of them actually wanted her help.

"Wrong foot, Mandy," she said when her youngest daughter slid her right foot into the left boot.

"I used to put my boots on the wrong feet," Davy admitted, "but that was when we first moved to Montana. We didn't wear boots in New Orleans 'cause we didn't have snow."

It was the first time she'd ever heard either of the boys mention their life before Josh had taken custody of them.

"Jingle bells, jingle bells, jingle all the way," Jenny sang at the top of her lungs as she slipped her arms into her jacket.

"Jingle bells, shotgun shells, rabbits all the way," Danny paraphrased just as loudly. This time both girls dissolved in laughter at his antics.

Their transportation was waiting just outside the back door when they stepped out into the frigid December morning. Chrysie stood there gawking. She couldn't help it. "It's awesome," she said.

"Yeah, it is pretty nifty, isn't it?" Josh agreed as he finished hitching the horses to the fancy sleigh.

"Where did you get it? It must have cost a fortune."

"I bought it from Pat Mechans. He has a ranch up north of here and he was getting rid of some of his equipment. This was the jewel of the sale. I had to outbid some rich guy who has a resort in upstate New York. He was mad as a bull stuck in a barbed-wire fence when I walked off with the prize."

It amazed her that Josh had spent that kind of money on a sleigh. But then, everything on the ranch seemed to be first class except the old and very small cabin.

Chrysie stopped to admire the horses as Josh helped the kids into the back of the sleigh and tucked a couple of heavy blankets around them.

Once that was done, he held out a hand. "Your carriage awaits, milady."

His gloved hand closed around hers, and her pulse

skyrocketed. She took deep breaths in an effort to stop the erratic beating of her heart. She refused to let him see the effect he had on her.

Once she was seated, Josh climbed in beside her and took the reins. A second later the horses were galloping across the snow, their heads high and their manes flowing behind them. Norman Rockwell couldn't have painted a scene more picturesque or evocative.

Josh slipped his right arm around her shoulders and pulled her closer. "Are you cold?"

"Freezing." On the outside. On the inside, the fear had subsided for the moment, leaving a river of molten gold.

IF PEOPLE ARE LUCKY, they have at least one perfect experience in their lives. Moments, sometimes hours, that are wrapped in silver and tied with a shimmering bow. An escapade where time doesn't exist, when laughter comes easily and hearts spill happiness that flows right down to the soul.

The sleigh ride was that kind of perfection for Chrysie.

The sky was a brilliant blue, the sun turning the snow-covered hills into a canvas of diamonds. But it was not only the exhilarating beauty or even the magic of sitting next to Josh that touched Chrysie's heart so profoundly. It was due in large part to seeing her daughters so genuinely happy, free, the way children should be.

Rousing choruses of "Frosty the Snowman," "Jingle Bells," "Rudolph" and "Joy to the World" were interspersed with laughter and ridiculous knock-knock jokes. And when the magnificent ride had stopped and they'd climbed from the sleigh, all four of the youngsters had taken off running through the snow like young fawns, awkward but joyous, frolicking in a world made just for them.

And, of course, the boundless energy had produced a friendly snowball fight. Well, at least reasonably friendly.

Chrysie had launched one technically perfect aerodynamic missile that had landed right in the middle of Josh's forehead. He got payback, of course, but that hadn't lessened her achievement.

And then she'd perched on a huge rock and watched while Josh had chopped down the tree that he'd insisted needed to be thinned from the crush of evergreens anyway.

He had shed his jacket before picking up the ax, and when he'd reared back and swung the tool, his muscles had flexed so that she could see the swell beneath his shirtsleeves. His virility was intoxicating, and she was a bit giddy by the time the tree was ready to be tied to the back of the sleigh.

It was indeed the perfect Christmas tree—for a

mansion. It was going to all but push out the windows and jut through the roof of Josh's cabin, a fact which obviously concerned no one but her.

But the sleigh ride, like all good things, was about to come to an end. The clomping sounds of the hooves slowed as the cabin came into view—the cabin and Josh's black pickup truck, which hadn't been there when they'd left. The golden warmth of perfection turned to an icy slush in Chrysie's veins.

Evelyn and Buck were no doubt returning the truck so that they could pick up their SUV and drive Chrysie, Jenny and Mandy back home. They'd expect her to be feeling well enough to stay on her own by now and, unlike the girls, they would know there were no roof problems and that the cabin wasn't flooded.

"Relax," Josh said. "I know what you're thinking, but it's under control."

Chrysie leaned close so that she could whisper to Josh without the children hearing. "You didn't tell the Millers why I'm really staying at your house, did you?"

"An abbreviated version of the truth."

"You promised you wouldn't tell a soul."

Josh took her hand and squeezed it. "All they know is that you need protection. They won't ask questions. They probably just want to see for themselves that you're okay."

Only she wasn't okay. With everyone who knew about her, the risks multiplied exponentially. Josh should understand that. She grew dizzy, felt as if she were on a spinning roller coaster that propelled her to the top only to plunge her to the depths a second later.

As marvelous as the sleigh ride had been, it was only an illusion in a world gone mad, the same as the kiss had been. The only thing that was real was the danger. She had to find a way to get away from Josh and out of Aohkii before it was too late.

THE MILLERS ONLY stayed a half hour and, as Josh had predicted, they hadn't asked questions. In fact, they'd delivered some of the toys the children had left in the cabin and assured Chrysie that the house would be waiting for her whenever she was ready to return. The Millers were good people.

When they'd left, the children had clamored to decorate the tree, but Josh had convinced them they should wait until they had purchased decorations. He'd promised they would make the forty-mile drive to the nearest Wal-Mart tomorrow to select their ornaments and then go out for hamburgers and fries before they showed up for Christmas play practice.

That arrangement let him maintain hero status while allowing him to watch the Packers game that afternoon without having to peer through the green needles.

He was stretched out on his worn recliner now, drinking a beer and second-guessing the coaches and officials. Jenny and Mandy were back in the bedroom, playing school. The boys were outside tossing a football around in the snow.

Chrysie had been working on her growing list about Jonathan, and surprisingly it had given her a few additional things to think about. The game broke for a string of commercials, and she put down her pencil. "Can we talk a minute?"

"Sure." Josh picked up the remote and muted the volume. "How's the list coming?"

"Now that I've thought about it, there were some changes in Jonathan's behavior over the months prior to his murder."

"What kind of changes?"

"He was edgier than usual after we moved into the new house."

"Why did you move?"

"Jonathan had always wanted to build a showplace. He kept at me until I agreed, though I didn't see how we could afford the house he wanted or the neighborhood."

"Then he must have been making good money."

"Yes, he'd struggled for years, but from the moment he'd become partners with Luisa Pellot, his career and income had taken off."

"How long had they been partners?"

"Only two years."

"Tell me about Luisa."

"She's one of the city's grand old dames. Her grandfather made and lost a couple of fortunes in his day, but Luisa made it on her own. Had it not been for her class and flair, she'd have been known as an ambulance chaser, but instead she was on every socialite's party list."

"A little stuffy, huh?"

"But in a nice sort of way. She was always terrific to me. I have to say, I liked her."

"How did she and Jonathan get along?"

"They had different styles as attorneys, so they sometimes disagreed over how to handle a particular case, but Jonathan loved the association he'd formed with her and he took advantage of all the social opportunities it provided. Overall, I'd say they had a pretty amiable working relationship."

"Was Jonathan on any kind of prescription drugs that might account for his edginess?"

"No. He never took so much as an aspirin. He was always on a health kick, worrying about eliminating sweets and carbs from his diet and working out religiously. Most likely his bad moods were the result of my asking for a divorce a few weeks before Mandy was born."

Josh dropped the remote to the table by his chair and turned to face her, his gaze boring into hers. "You never mentioned that you'd asked for a divorce."

Chrysie pulled one leg up onto the sofa with her,

tucking it under her. She hadn't mentioned it because it was just one more thing that made her look guilty. Judging from Josh's reaction, it had probably been a mistake to mention it now. "It had no bearing on anything," she said, still skirting the issue.

"The police probably didn't see it that way."

"I didn't tell them."

"No, but I'm sure someone they questioned did. His secretary girlfriend. Maybe his partner. So what's the story?"

"The marriage wasn't working. Actually, it never had. We had too much going against us from the very first."

"So why did you get married?"

"It was a spur-of-the-moment decision. I'd only known him a couple of weeks when we flew together to Vegas for a psychologist's conference. I was infatuated with Jonathan, probably because he was so different from me. He was boisterous and outgoing where I was quiet and inhibited."

Josh nodded. "They say opposites attract."

"True, but that doesn't mean they can live together in harmony, especially if the values and backgrounds are also opposite."

"What was your background?" Josh asked.

"It doesn't really matter does it?"

"It could."

Chrysie knotted and unknotted her hands, feeling

the pressure build inside her the way it always did when she ventured too far into her past.

"My mother died when I was ten, and I went to live with a very rich uncle whose wife hated having me around. I tried, but nothing I ever did suited her."

"Where was your father?"

"Never had one. My mother was a free spirit. A nymphomaniac, according to my aunt. Anyway, all I knew officially was that he was never part of our lives."

"That's tough. It could be that your mother never told him about you."

"That's quite possible. I remember her boyfriends coming to the house, but I don't remember any of them staying in the picture for very long."

"What was Jonathan's background?"

"He was one of six children. His father was a truck driver until he wrecked his rig and banged up his knee so badly that he couldn't drive the distances anymore. His wife picked that time to jump ship, taking her two daughters with her. Jonathan was left with three younger brothers and his alcoholic father."

"Sounds as if you both had it rough growing up."

"But it affected us differently. I chose a career in psychology—an effort to figure out myself, I'm sure. Jonathan's goal in life was to make as much money as he could as fast as he could and then impress the hell out of people who couldn't have cared less."

"When did you decide the infatuation wasn't enough?"

"About the time I got pregnant with Mandy. That was four years into the marriage. I'm not blaming Jonathan for the marriage not working. It's just the infatuation died, and there wasn't any real love to hold the marriage together."

The game was back on TV, but Jonathan wasn't watching it. He raked his hair off his forehead, then pulled his recliner to an upright position. "I'd like to take a look at the additions to your list," he said.

"There's not much there other than what I've already told you." She handed him the notebook but wasn't ready to let the conversation go. "You don't think the break-in or the murder were random acts, do you?"

"I think there's a good chance they weren't, but I need a lot more information before I can prove that."

"There is no more information."

"Oh, it's out there. We just don't have it yet."

"What's our next move?"

"I'm gathering some mug shots of Houston criminals for you to take a look at and I'm going to Houston to do a little investigating on my own."

She swallowed hard, sure she couldn't have heard him right. But the determined jut of his chin and the hard lines in his face assured her she had. "How long do you think it will be before the cops show up at this door once the Houston police find out that you're there?"

"They won't find out."

"Why are you doing this, Josh? You're the sheriff. Why risk your job for me when you hardly know me?"

"I like living on the edge." He scooted back in his chair and took a long sip of his beer. "And you make good pancakes."

CHRYSIE'S NERVES WERE rattling like ghost chains in a haunted house by midmorning on Monday, though thankfully Josh wasn't flying to Houston until the following morning. She had no idea what he was doing today, except that he'd driven Jenny, Davy and Danny to the consolidated elementary school in the borrowed SUV, leaving Chrysie and Mandy on the ranch with Cougar to keep them company.

She'd tried to think of an excuse to keep Jenny home from school today just in case she found the opportunity to make a run for it but decided Josh would see right through the ruse. Better to wait until tomorrow, after he'd left for Houston and the children had returned from school.

Chrysie poured another cup of coffee. Cougar lumbered in from the den, where he'd been watching cable news for the last half hour.

"It's started to snow and there's lots more on the way," he commented.

"Did you catch a weather forecast?"

"Nope. Don't need 'em. My bones are a better forecaster anyway. They always know when a storm's a-movin' in. Wouldn't surprise me none to have blizzard conditions by morning."

It would be her first major winter storm, and the timing couldn't be worse. "Do they cancel flights when there's a blizzard?"

"If it's bad enough, they cancel everything."

That was good and bad. She couldn't leave, but neither could Josh, so he wouldn't be stirring up trouble in Houston. She stared out the window. It was overcast and glum but barely snowing. If a blizzard was in the forecast, she was pretty sure Josh would cancel their shopping trip. The play rehearsal might be cancelled, as well, though she'd already learned that people in Montana didn't like canceling anything due to snow.

It was going to be a long day if she didn't find something to keep her busy. She rummaged through the cupboards to see if Josh had the ingredients for homemade cookies. Dr. Cassandra Harwell had never baked. Chrysie Atwater had become pretty good at it. She located the necessities and discovered she even had choices.

"What's your preference, Cougar, oatmeal-raisin, sugar or peanut-butter cookies?"

"Homemade?"

"Is there any other kind?"

"Only store-bought around my house."

"Then this is your lucky day."

"'Bout time I had one of those." He grinned. "I'm not picky. I'll eat any of 'em, but oatmeal and peanut butter are my favorite."

"Maybe I'll bake both."

In minutes she was elbow-deep in cookie dough and her black sweatshirt was sprinkled with flour. Cougar's cell phone made a tinkling sound that reminded her of the ice-cream truck that had gone through their neighborhood back before her mother had died. He yelled a hello into it, then stepped out onto the back porch to spit and get a better connection. The heat from the oven blasted into Chrysie's face as she pushed the first filled cookie sheet onto the top shelf.

When she closed it, a draft of cold air hit her from behind. She turned to see if Cougar had come in and left the back door open. It was closed tight, and Cougar was still on the phone. From the looks of his red face, he was having an argument with the caller.

Wind fluttered the newspaper Cougar had left on the kitchen table. Cougar must have opened a window somewhere. She went to check it out.

The front door was wide-open. Chrysie called for Mandy. There was no answer. Panic swelled to suffocating proportions before Chrysie caught a glimpse of her young daughter, outside and nearly to the garage, stamping about in Chrysie's boots that were sizes too big for her.

Mandy had pulled on her jacket but not the hood, and snow was sticking to her blond hair and giving her the appearance of one of those snow angels they sold in the Christmas stores.

Chrysie grabbed her own jacket and pushed through the front door. She was greeted by a bracing gust of wind. She hugged herself, made a megaphone of her right hand and yelled. "Mandy. Maaaandy!"

Mandy either didn't hear the call in the wind or pretended not to. Chrysie stuck her feet into the boots Cougar had left on the front porch and went sloshing through the snow to get her daughter.

When she caught up with her, she took her hand. "You know you're not supposed to go outside without my permission."

"I want to see the sleigh."

"That's no reason for coming outside without permission."

"Can we go see it, please?"

"Not now. I have cookies in the oven. When they're done, we'll come outside for a few minutes."

Chrysie turned back, expecting to see Cougar tramping through the snow after them. Instead she saw a black car heading down the hilly tree-lined road to the house. She'd only gotten a glimpse before the car disappeared in a curve in the road, but she'd seen enough to know it wasn't the truck."

Apprehension burned in her chest, and impulsively she swooped Mandy into her arms and took cover inside the garage. It was a neighbor, she told herself, just someone stopping by to see Josh. But the fear persisted, swelling with every second of waiting.

She left the door open a crack so that a slanted line of light crept into the damp space. She watched through the opening as the car reappeared and jerked to a stop right at the end of the driveway.

"I'm cold. Let's go get cookies, Mommy."

"In a minute." But her words felt as icy as the vapor that escaped her lips as she watched two men climb from the vehicle. The first turned toward her before starting up the walk. It had been three years, but recognition was immediate and sure.

Jonathan's killers had come calling again.

Chapter Nine

Chrysie felt as if she were caught in an avalanche, careening down a mountain with nothing to grab hold of to break the fall. Crushing Mandy to her chest, she fell against the inside wall of the beamed garage.

Mandy squirmed and tried to wiggle from her arms. Chrysie held her all the tighter. Her assumption that the contemptible thugs wanted her for a scapegoat was obviously flawed. They wanted her dead. Why else would they be here?

The answer slammed into her overwrought brain: they'd needed her alive then, but they didn't need her alive now. The police were already firmly convinced that she was Jonathan's killer, and if she showed up dead on some ranch in Montana, it would just allow them to consider the case closed.

Mandy pressed her little hands against Chrysie's cheeks. "I wanna ride in the sleigh."

"Not now, Mandy." Chrysie turned away from the

door, looking around as her eyes adjusted to the dim light. A vintage Chevrolet on blocks occupied the right half of the structure, and the sleigh took up the left. Behind them were a workbench, the four-wheeler with parts to the engine lying on the floor beside it and a shiny two-seated snowmobile that looked to be brand-new.

"Where're the horses?" Mandy asked.

"In the pasture," Chrysie whispered. She scanned the garage looking for a place to hide and wondering if she dared stay here. Would the men leave when they didn't find her and Mandy in the house? Or would they search the garage next?

Her gut instinct was to just take off running, but how fast could she run carrying Mandy and sloshing through the snow?

Her gaze fixed on the snowmobile. She'd only ridden a snowmobile once, and that had been on a ski trip back when she was in college. The ride had ended in disaster when she'd buried the vehicle in a snowdrift and it had taken two men to pull it out.

A blast of gunfire shattered the quiet. Chrysie held her breath, paralyzed by a new wave of terror. Had Cougar fired that shot? Or was he dead, lying in the cabin in a pool of blood the way Jonathan had been? The image spurred her to action.

She kicked open the door, then ran to the back of the garage, grabbing one of the blankets from the sleigh as she raced by it. Cocooning Mandy in the blanket, she tucked her into the small passenger seat.

She pushed the machine out the door, then jumped on board and gunned the engine. The machine lurched forward, then took off on a jerky path across the snow.

Chrysie didn't dare look back as she gained more control of the snowmobile and sped across the open fields and into the hilly area just behind the house. If she could disappear fast enough, the monsters might not even see her escape.

That hope died when she heard a round of gunfire and saw a bullet ricochet off a huge boulder just a few feet ahead of her.

She topped a hill and started down it, hoping that put her out of the men's sight, though she couldn't be sure. All she could do was drive as fast as she could and hope she didn't smash the vehicle into a rock or tree or skid into a snowbank.

The icy wind cut through her. She didn't mind it for herself but worried for Mandy. The girl must think her mother had totally lost her mind, but to her credit, she wasn't screaming or crying.

Chrysie was going way too fast, but she didn't dare slow down. The men couldn't have followed her in their car, but if they'd thought of it, they might have commandeered a couple of Josh's horses. Of course, they'd have had to find them first.

She kept driving, over one hill and down another,

past pine trees and along the banks of creeks, around boulders and fallen limbs. At one point a deer crossed a few feet in front of them. Mandy squealed her pleasure.

Finally, cold to the bone, Chrysie slowed and studied her surroundings. There was nothing but acres of snow-covered terrain, and all of it looked pretty much the same for as far as she could see. It was probably near noon, but she couldn't be sure since she'd taken off her watch when she'd started kneading cookie dough, and the sun had disappeared behind layers of low clouds.

There was no sign that they were being followed. She sucked in a deep breath, then started shaking as a new terror took hold in her brain. What about Jenny? What if the murderous thugs showed up at her school and kidnapped her? What if they…?

Mandy's scream snapped her to attention.

They were headed right for a cluster of towering pine trees. Chrysie spun the steering wheel, missing the trees but sending the snowmobile into a roll. When it stopped moving, they were buried in a snowdrift.

Chrysie's ears were ringing when she reached for Mandy. "Are you okay?"

"I've got snow in my eyes."

"Me, too, baby. Me, too." Chrysie bit back tears as she lifted Mandy out of the snow and carried her back to the shelter of the trees. Not that the pines provided much shelter from the cold or the dampness.

But at least they were alive. She wondered if that were true of Cougar.

But her real fears were for Jenny. If only she could talk to Josh. He'd go to school, pick up Jenny and keep her safe. And then he'd find a way to rescue her and Mandy. Or maybe he'd just get shot by the killers, too.

"Wanna go home," Mandy said.

"We will soon, sweetie." That just might be the cruelest lie she'd ever told.

JOSH BALANCED the phone between his chin and shoulder and scribbled down the pertinent details he'd just learned about Jonathan Harwell's past—facts he'd be willing to bet that Chrysie had never heard. "I knew I could count on you, Grecco."

"Hey, what are buds for? So why are you so concerned with a dead guy?"

"Some dead men cast a long shadow."

"That might be true, but I know you too well to think you're wasting time chasing shadows."

"I'll fill you in once I get to Houston."

"I'll hold you to that."

Eager to share his new knowledge with Chrysie, Josh broke the connection and punched in his home phone number. He hung up after the tenth ring. They must have gone outside for some fresh air and exercise before the storm came in. He rang Cougar's cell number. After the third ring, the acid started gnawing away at the lining of Josh's stomach.

He was worrying for nothing. Cougar wasn't as young and strong as he used to be, but he was as dependable as they came. Chrysie and Mandy were in good hands with him. But that reassurance turned sour when a computerized voice cut in asking Josh if he'd like to leave a message. He left one, a string of curses that did nothing toward relieving his anxiety.

Apprehension was kicking around inside him big-time as he punched in Chrysie's cell phone number. Still no answer. Damn. He'd thought he and Chrysie were on the same page now, but he might have gotten those signals all wrong. She could have found some way to run again—but not without Jenny.

He called the elementary school and had them see if Jenny Atwater had been checked out of school. They wouldn't have given that information out to just anyone. Being sheriff carried its privileges.

Jenny was still at school, and there was no way Chrysie had taken off without her. She had to be at the ranch with Mandy and Cougar. Maybe the approaching storm had messed up the phone service. Maybe—

He grabbed his jacket and keys and raced for the door of his office, kicking a chair out of his way rather than going around it.

In a matter of seconds he was speeding down the highway with his portable lights flashing red and blue and his siren blaring. He tried all the numbers again, struggling to convince himself there was a logical reason for not reaching them, though by now he knew there wasn't. The only explanation was that the sons of bitches who'd killed Jonathan Harwell had shown up at the ranch.

Josh's chest felt as if someone were smashing it with a baseball bat. He'd run along the edge all his life, driven in the fast lane, flirted with danger as if he couldn't get enough of it. But nothing had ever scared him the way he was scared right now. He'd blow their evil friggin' heads off if they'd laid a hand on Chrysie or Mandy.

He made a couple of calls to ensure the safety of Jenny and the boys while he sped to his ranch.

The snow had started to fall a lot harder by the time Josh slammed on his brakes in front of his cabin. Black clouds of swirling smoke poured though the open front door, and the acrid smell of burned food seemed to peel the skin from his nostrils as he drew his gun and raced up the path and into the house.

Wary, he kept his back to the wall as he yelled for Chrysie and Cougar and searched the house. He worked his way to the kitchen and turned off the oven. Wherever they'd gone, they'd left in a hurry.

Coughing, he stepped to the back door to escape the blinding, choking smoke. That's when he saw the blood, a stream of it working its way across the porch and down the back steps, deep red as it cut a path through the snow. And just to the right of the door he saw Cougar, lying facedown in a sticky crimson pool, his cell phone at the tips of his outstretched fingers.

Josh's hands shook as he knelt beside the man, and even as he checked Cougar's weak pulse, he called for an ambulance. He tried to get Cougar to tell him what had happened to Chrysie and Mandy, but the deputy was unconscious and probably on the brink of death. He'd lost too much blood.

There was nothing he could do for Cougar, but he prayed that wouldn't be true of Chrysie and Mandy. After bringing the injured man inside he raced around the outside of the house. Any tracks the killers had left would be covered soon.

He found tire tracks of a car and remnants of two sets of large footprints going to and from the house. None of the prints belonged to either Chrysie or Mandy, and there was no sign of anything having been dragged.

But there were other prints, as well, going to and from the garage, and some of them appeared to belong to Chrysie and Mandy.

He raced to the garage, afraid of what he might find, barely able to breathe until he saw the snowmobile tracks. His pulse skyrocketed. The tracks had to mean that Chrysie and Mandy had escaped. Unable to follow, the men would have taken the car and driven away.

But if Chrysie and Mandy were in the snowmobile, they could be anywhere. He had to find them before the snow covered the tracks. If they were stranded a night in the predicted blizzard...

He spun around and stared at the four-wheeler with parts of the engine still scattered about the floor. He cursed himself for leaving it in that condition, then realized that had he not, the men who'd shot Cougar would have used it to give Chrysie chase.

Working at lightning speed, he screwed the parts back in place and revved the engine. It sputtered but finally came to life. Josh gunned the accelerator and took off, following the trail left by the snowmobile.

Dozens of frightening scenarios still lurked at the corners of his mind. He pushed them away. He had to believe Chrysie and Mandy had somehow escaped and that he'd find them before it was too late. The frigid wind hit him in the face as he bounced across the snow, going airborne as he sped across one hill after another.

He dodged a bull that refused to move and stirred up a moose that disappeared into the heavily wooded area just north of the creek. The snow was falling harder now, making it difficult to see and almost impossible to follow the tracks.

Finally he lost the tracks completely. Josh stopped and looked around. If he just drove on blindly, he might be going in the opposite direction. He needed help, needed searchers to comb the area. Needed a helicopter search, but even if he could get someone to go up, he doubted how much the rescuers could see in the worsening storm.

He'd promised he could keep Chrysie and the girls safe, but he'd failed them. Now she and Mandy were lost on his ranch, with a blizzard coming on fast. He buried his head in his hand as the pressure swelled between his temples. He had to do something.

His hand was on the throttle when he heard the faint sound of "Jingle Bells" floating along on the piercing wind. The song stopped as he slid off the four-wheeler, yelling their names. "Mandy! Maaaandy? Chrysie!"

"Josh!"

His heart slammed against his rib cage. He took off running toward the sound. Chrysie was sitting under a pine tree, cuddling Mandy, who was wrapped up like an Indian papoose in the old wool blanket from the sleigh. He fell to his knees beside them.

"They were here," Chrysie said shakily through lips that were starting to turn blue.

"I know." Josh tried to say more, but words just wouldn't come. Not yet. He was shaken all the way to his soul. He'd come too close to losing Chrysie, and the intensity of his relief was almost as frightening as the situation.

"I wanna go home," Mandy said.

"And that's where we're going," he said. He

took Mandy from Chrysie's arms and helped Chrysie to her feet.

"Where's Jenny?" Chrysie whispered.

"She's fine. She and the boys are both fine. I made sure of that."

"And Cougar?"

"He's alive." He let it go at that, and Chrysie didn't ask for more. There would be a lot to talk about later. Plans to make. Killers to catch. Blame to accept.

But right now just knowing Chrysie and Mandy were safe was enough for him.

THEY'D LEFT THE windows and doors open all afternoon, let the blustery winds from the storm suck the smoke from the house. The bedrooms had fared well, but the smoke had saturated walls and furniture in the kitchen and den, and even now that it was near midnight, the den still carried a burning stench.

He'd put the boys' sleeping bags on the floor beside the bunk beds. He wasn't sure where he'd sleep—or if he'd sleep.

Josh held the phone in his right hand and a cup of steaming coffee in his left while he waited for his brother to pick up on the other end. He didn't know how he'd explain all of this to Logan in a phone conversation, but he'd have to manage, since he was planning to ask a major favor.

"Hello, Josh."

"Hope I didn't interrupt anything."

"At one in the morning?"

"Sorry. It's not quite that late here."

"So does this late-night call have anything to do with the complications you mentioned the other day?"

"Yeah, and things are getting more complicated by the minute. Which is why I have a favor to ask."

"Anything. You know that."

"In that case, look for a noisy menagerie to arrive in New Orleans as soon as the storm's over and our airport reopens. You'll have to pick them up, of course."

"Whoa. Menagerie?"

"Four children under the age of seven."

"Would that include my adorable nephews?"

"Yes, and two just as adorable little girls, ages five and three."

"Okay, big brother, start talking. Give me the whole scoop."

"Well, there's this woman...."

"Isn't there always?"

NOT ONLY HAD LOGAN agreed to take Chrysie and the children and keep them safe for a few days, but talking to him had helped Josh clarify a few things in his own mind, especially about how the killers had tracked Chrysie to Aohkii.

He'd have to play this very carefully from here on out, but he knew what he had to do. He'd dig as deeply as he needed into Jonathan Harwell's past and find out exactly what had led to the man's murder. And when he discovered the motive behind the killing, he'd know the identity of the killers.

It was the only way to prove Chrysie's innocence, the only way to free her from the danger that had entrapped her and the girls for three long years.

He finished his coffee, checked on the kids, then noticed the light was still shining beneath the door to Chrysie's bedroom. Obviously she couldn't sleep either. He tiptoed to the door and knocked softly.

"Come in," she whispered, opening the door for him.

She was a vision in a pale pink nightshirt that fell just above her knees. She looked soft and feminine and incredibly vulnerable, and he hated thinking of all she'd been through that day.

Her short blond hair was still wet from the shower. She pushed it back from her face and tucked it behind her ears. "Have you heard anything more on Cougar's condition?"

"He made it though surgery. He's still on the critical list. The doctor told Cougar's wife that if he makes it through the next twenty-four hours, he has a good chance of making a full recovery."

"Thank God."

She walked to the window and stared out into the storm that was still rattling the windows and blowing snow against the panes. "You should never have brought me here, Josh. If you hadn't, Cougar wouldn't be fighting for his life."

The pain bled through her voice. Josh could stand it no more. He walked up behind her and put his arms about her waist. "None of this is your fault, Chrysie."

"I should have told the police the truth from the beginning. They might have caught the killers and put them behind bars."

"Or they might have killed you just as they threatened." He tugged her around to face him. Her eyes were moist. "Those guys are thugs, but they're not invincible. We'll stop them, and you and the girls will be free to live your lives."

"You make it sound easy."

"All in a day's work." He was striving to lighten the moment but didn't pull it off. He took her hands in his. "We can do this, Chrysie. I'll need your help, but we can do it."

She shook her head. "It's too dangerous and you've done enough. I can't let you do more. I can't keep risking the girls' lives."

"So what are you suggesting? That we just hand the victory to those two-bit hoodlums?"

"I've made up my mind, Josh. It's over. I'm turning myself in to the Houston police." She turned away and wiped a tear from her eye. "In fact, I've already called them."

Chapter Ten

Josh reeled at Chrysie's statement. "How could you do something like that without talking to me first?"

"This isn't about you, Josh. It's about me and my children. Mandy could have been killed today. I can't keep gambling with their lives."

"And just how will your being in jail make them safer?"

"I talked to Detective Hernandez. He promised me that he'd see they were protected while he investigated my story. I have no choice but to believe him."

"Detective Juan Hernandez?"

"Yes. Do you know him?"

"He's the same cop I talked to when I called to ask about Dr. Cassandra Harwell." Josh paced the room. It seemed a lifetime ago that he'd made that call. Cassandra Harwell had been a virtual stranger. It was difficult to justify what he'd heard about that woman with the young, vulnerable mother who'd moved into his home, into his heart. Hell, it was difficult to justify his own actions.

He was the sheriff. He should have turned Chrysie in to the Houston Police Department himself. Now here he was ready to do anything necessary to keep her from turning herself in.

Chrysie put her hand on his arm. "I appreciate what you've done, Josh, but I've made my decision."

And he'd made his. He wrapped his fingers around her arms and held her at arm's length, facing him. "I can't let you do this, Chrysie—or should I call you Cassandra now?"

"No, the name change would only confuse Jenny and Mandy more."

She tried to walk away from him. His grip tightened. "Listen to me. I know damn well that the buddies I talked with didn't do anything to alert the killers that you were here. But someone did. And the only other person it could have been was Detective Hernandez or someone he told that I'd called."

Her eyes narrowed. "You surely don't think the men who killed Jonathan and shot Cougar were cops?"

"I don't know what to think, but I can assure you stranger things have happened. Wearing a badge doesn't guarantee morality."

She shuddered, and he pulled her into his arms and buried his face in her sweet-smelling hair.

"They know I'm here," she whispered. "They'll come back."

"Let them. We won't be anywhere around." He lifted her chin so that he could look into her eyes. Her fear was right there, transparent, heart-wrenching. "As soon as the storm is over, we're flying to New Orleans," he assured her. "I've already talked to my brother, Logan. He and his wife will take you and all four of the children and make sure you stay safe."

"Did you tell him—"

Josh interrupted her with a finger to her lips. "I told Logan everything. I'm entrusting him with the safety of you and the children. I owed him the truth."

"But the police know I'm with you. If they are behind this, they may check out your family if I don't show up in Houston and they don't find me here."

"You're starting to think like a cop."

"That's a sickening thought."

"Not necessarily. Most of us toe the line. We may waver occasionally, but we don't jump sides."

"What if the killers go to your brother?"

"He's chartering a plane and planning a secret vacation until this thing is settled and the thugs are behind bars. And don't worry—on the off chance the killers should find him, he'll have enough body-guards to ensure everyone's safety, the way I should have ensured yours."

"I have some money," she said, "but I don't know if I have enough to cover all of that."

"Money isn't an issue." Funny thing about money. It never meant a thing to him until he needed it. He tugged her to the bed, dropped down to the edge and pulled her down beside him. "Now that you're about to be tossed into the McCain clan, there are probably a few things I should tell you about myself—and my family."

EVERY MUSCLE IN Chrysie's body ached from the wild ride on the snowmobile. The fear was so real it permeated her very being. Her head was so stopped up she could barely breathe in spite of the nose spray she'd been overdosing on all evening, and her throat felt as if it had been scratched with a rusty nail.

All that, and still she listened with rapt attention as Josh described his life as the oldest and very rebellious son of one of the richest men in New Orleans.

"Dad and I never agreed on anything," Josh said. "He was all about money and power. I was convinced he was pompous and greedy and I wanted no part of the life he had planned for me."

"What did you want to be?"

"A cop, right from the first time I caught an old Dirty Harry movie on TV."

"And he protested?"

"Oh, he did more than protest. He paid off the

right people and saw to it that I failed my physical though I was in great shape. He thought that would push me into the family business."

"What did you do?"

"Flunked out of college and got in with the wrong crowd. I hung out in bars, partied with young coeds, generally made a mess of my life in the guise of punishing him."

"How did your mother feel about that?"

"It just about killed her. I hate that now, but then I was too into my own self-destruction to care much about anybody else. I'm not trying to condone my actions. I'm just telling you the way it was. It kind of explains me, I guess."

Josh McCain had been an enigma since the moment they'd met. This didn't explain him, but it helped her see his fierce determination to go at this his way and his willingness to take a chance on her instead of turning her in immediately.

"I saw men younger than me lose their life to drugs," Josh continued. "And the dealers were never satisfied. They kept going after younger and younger kids, getting them hooked, ruining their lives. I'd finally had enough. I went to the narcs and told them I'd deliver the biggest dealers in the area to them as long as we did it on my terms."

"You squealed on drug dealers?"

"I went further than that. I helped set up the sting."

"I can't believe the dealers let you live."

"They didn't. I was killed by police fire in the shoot-out that accompanied the operation. I was pronounced dead, and Josh McCain was buried in a closed casket."

No wonder he'd picked up on her being on the run so quickly. He'd been on the run himself, right down to the alias. But he hadn't had two children with him at the time. Apparently they'd come later. And he had a brother he could count on. "Your family must have known you weren't really dead."

"Not then. Fake grief is too easy to see through, and I couldn't take a chance that they'd give me away. It was tough not telling Logan or Mom, but I think I got some kind of sick satisfaction for having my father think I was dead. I'm not happy about those feelings, but the enmity between us had run too deep."

"Did you go into witness protection?"

"I was offered protective custody. I turned them down, figured I'd do better on my own. So I ended up here in Montana as Josh Morgan. I worked for a while, then used some of the money I'd managed to smuggle out with me and bought this ranch."

"Where do Danny and Davy fit into all of this?"

"That's another story, a long story, for a better day. In fact, I should let my brother's wife tell you about them. Rachel and Logan are the reason they're alive and with me today. Believe me when I say you and our four children could not be in better hands than theirs."

She'd love to know the rest of the story, but her mind was teeming now with all the things that had happened today and all she'd heard tonight. It was a marvel that she'd ended up in Aohkii, a miracle that she'd tangled with Josh over a Christmas tree.

But neither that nor his own troubled past adequately explained the attraction that had simmered between them from the very first.

"You need to get some rest," Josh said. "We'll have to leave the second the storm breaks and the roads are cleared, but don't worry about packing. Just throw the necessities together, and Logan can arrange to have whatever you need delivered."

"Just like the lives of the rich and famous."

"Sort of, but you'll never get that feeling with Rachel and Logan."

He stood and walked to the door. She followed him. Might as well level with him now. "I appreciate your offer of protection for the girls, but I won't be going to your brother's with them."

Irritation flashed in his dark eyes. "Did you hear anything I said about Detective Hernandez?"

"I heard." She leaned against the door frame. "I'm not turning myself in to the police. I'm going with you. I know Jonathan better than anyone. If you're investigating his murder, I should be there to help."

"No way."

"Sorry, Sheriff, you may be as stubborn as any Louisiana or Montana man who ever ate a crawfish or branded a cow. But I'm a Texan and a woman. This is one argument you are not going to win."

She expected him to storm away, but he lingered, and what she saw in his eyes sent a surge of passion through her that was so consuming she grew dizzy in its wake.

Josh took her in his arms, and once their lips met, there was no holding back. He kissed her over and over, coming up for breath only to find her lips again.

When he finally pulled away, she sank back against the door frame, too weak to stand on her own.

"I'd better go," he said, "while I still can."

She knew she should let him walk away. She was tired and achy. He had to be exhausted, as well. Only she would climb into a soft, warm bed—his bed— while he would crawl into a bag on a cold floor in a room that still reeked of smoke.

"Wait."

He turned and looked back at her, and her pulse took a traitorous leap. "You should sleep in a full-size bed tonight."

His brow arched questioningly. "There's only one."

"I know, but it's big enough for two."

He shook his head. "You may be a stubborn woman, Chrysie Atwater, but I'm a man. If I crawl between the sheets with you, I'll do more than sleep."

She didn't say a word, just opened the door wide and ushered him back inside.

IT HAD BEEN OVER three years since Chrysie had been with a man. She'd have expected it to be awkward after so long a time, but her body was hot with desire as he crawled into bed beside her.

Josh stretched out next to her and let his fingers tangle in the short locks of hair that hugged her right cheek. "I love all those little golden curls."

"So you have a weakness for blondes, do you?"

"I do now."

"Have you slept with lots of women?"

"I don't count." He kissed her lips, then let his mouth wander to the tip of her nose and her forehead. "Is that what we're doing, Chrysie? Sleeping together?"

"What else would you call this?"

"Making love with a woman who's turned my life upside down."

He smiled, and it went all through her, warming places that she'd barely known existed before him. "I don't understand it," she said. "I've worked on building barriers around me and my girls for three years, thought they were invincible, and you just slipped right through as if they were made of whipped cream."

"It's the jeans and boots," he teased. "Women can't resist a cowboy."

"I'm from Texas. I've resisted plenty of cowboys, the urban and the authentic."

"Chemistry happens. Maybe we're meant to be." He kissed her again, then fit his arm around her shoulders and rolled her closer. "I'm crazy about you, Chrysie. You, your girls, the way you hold everything together no matter how much trouble batters you around."

"It's an act," she said. "I'm scared most of the time."

"I know, but you don't let the fear win, and that turns me on, too." He kissed her again. "How long do we have to talk?"

"Are you just talking to appease me?"

"I love to talk to you, just not right now." He pulled her so close she felt his erection against her thighs. She trembled and fit herself so closely against his body it would have been difficult to pass a feather between them.

He reached beneath her nightshirt and fumbled with the buttons. She started to help him but decided against it. She wanted this to last, ached to savor every moment of the first time with Josh McCain. Life was too uncertain to let even a moment of pleasure go to waste.

She slipped her hands between his legs and tucked them inside his briefs as he undid the last button and pushed the nightshirt from her shoulders. He moaned and took her right nipple in his mouth, sucking and massaging it with his tongue, turning her on to the point that she felt a trickle of hot moisture between her thighs.

"Are you ready?" he whispered, his breath hot on her already burning flesh.

"Yes. Oh, yes."

He wiggled out of his briefs, finally naked beside her. She stared, unable to look away as her hunger for him swelled out of control. He was magnificent. All of him. Strong chest dotted with a generous sprinkling of dark hairs. Flat, hard stomach. Strong, tanned, manly thighs. And an erection like none she'd ever seen.

Josh took her hands in his and guided her fingers over her most private parts. They explored her body hand in hand, both their fingers slipping inside her, touching and feeling and discovering every erogenous nerve. This was new for her, incredibly hot, powerfully seductive.

She came in his hand, but that didn't lessen the surge of desire when he fit her fingers around the long, hard length of him. She guided him into her, then moaned from the thrill of it as he pushed and throbbed deep inside her.

It happened too fast then, white-hot desire surging through her until she felt her pounding heart might break right through the walls of her chest. She heard his short, quick gasps for breath and felt the blood rushing through his shaft and then they exploded together. One quick, powerful lunge and it was all over.

And yet it wasn't. She was changed in ways she didn't understand. All she knew was that this was far more than two people reaching out to each other in a storm of danger.

Maybe not love. She still wasn't sure what that meant. But theirs was a connection that defied all odds, and that was enough for her. At least it was enough for now.

That was the last thought she remembered before exhaustion took hold and she fell asleep in Josh's arms.

MAC BUCKLEY refilled his glass, pouring the cheap liquor to the rim. He was drunk. Who gave a dog's behind? There was nothing to do anyway but sit out the storm in this sorry, freezing motel that had lost power hours ago.

Sean was still sober. That was his problem, except that Sean kept making it Mac's by wanting to talk about the way they'd screwed up today.

Sean was playing with the flashlight now, shining it around the room, trying to find scurrying cockroaches and squash their guts all over the dingy carpet. Every now and then the beam swiped over Sean's face, giving his ugly mug an eerie glow that made him look like a zombie from a freak show.

"She'll be mad as hell," Sean said.

"We're up here in a blizzard. What does she expect?"

"She don't expect us to go shooting a man for no cause, the way you did."

Mac downed about a third of his drink. "I had cause. He had a gun on his hip."

"Yeah, well, we may find ourselves with a bullet in the back if we don't take out Cassandra Harwell soon."

"She'd'a been dead long ago if it was up to me."

"Nothing's up to you. You're paid to do a job, that's all."

Mac finished his drink and poured another. He didn't see what Sean or the boss woman was all steamed about. Cassandra had been running around free for three years. What difference could one more day make?

His cell phone rang, startling him so that he spilled half his drink down the front of his shirt. Mac yanked the handkerchief from his back pocket and started dabbing at his shirt. Sean grabbed for the phone.

It was the boss. No one else made Sean sweat bullets the way he was doing right now. Mac staggered to the bed and fell across it.

"You better lay off that booze," Sean said when he'd broken the connection. "We got a job to do first thing in the morning."

"There's a friggin' blizzard. Did you tell her that?"

"She knows. Says it will be over by morning. And we got to act fast."

"What's the hurry?"

"Cassandra contacted the Houston police tonight. She's flying there tomorrow and turning herself in, only we got to make sure that she never catches that plane."

Mac's head rolled off the pillow. Good thing it was tomorrow he was supposed to pull the trigger, 'cause tonight he was dead drunk.

CHRYSIE WOKE THE next morning to sun streaming through the frosted windows, an ear-splitting racket—and an empty bed. She rolled onto the pillow Josh had slept on, buried her nose it and tried to pick up his scent.

Instead she coughed, releasing what felt like a ton of germs into the bed. The cold that had been coming on last night was now full-blown. She sniffed and tried to pull some air into her stopped-up nostrils while she gingerly slid her legs over the side of the bed.

Her muscles protested even that bit of movement. Riding a bucking snowmobile had taken its toll. So had sex, but the ache between her thighs was a much easier pain to bear. She slid her feet into her fur-lined slippers and pulled on her warm flannel robe.

She was still tying it when the door opened behind her and Josh walked it. He was already dressed in jeans and a sweatshirt and had his black parka slung over his shoulder.

"You're awake. Good."

"How could I not be awake with all that racket outside the window?"

"That's my neighbor. Skaggs's roads are always the first ones cleared after a storm. When he finishes plowing his, he hits mine. We tease him, tell him he'd rather plow than screw—sorry, Montana guy talk."

"So I gathered." No morning kiss. She wondered if he was going to pretend last night never happened or if he just had other things on his mind. She turned to check the time, but the crumpled edge of the blanket blocked her view. "What time is it?"

"Eight-thirty."

"You're kidding, right?"

"Nope. You had a rough time of it yesterday. I figured you needed the sleep."

"But the children need breakfast and…"

"I gave them cereal. They're fine and way ahead of you. They're dressed and ready to go catch a plane."

Chrysie placed her fingers on her suddenly throbbing temples. When Josh made up his mind to do something, he wasted no time. "Surely the main roads haven't been cleared yet."

"No, but they will be soon."

"What time do you plan on leaving for the airport?"

"As soon as you're ready. The boys and I are packed."

"I have to talk to Jenny and Mandy and prepare

them for this. Your brother and his wife may be wonderful people, but they're strangers to the girls."

"I already told them about the vacation, and now Danny and Davy are telling them how much fun they're going to have. All four are rarin' to go."

Just like that. She wanted this. Wanted the girls safe and wanted the chance to find out why Jonathan had been murdered. Wanted to prove her innocence and give the girls a real life.

She wanted it, and yet she had a terrifying feeling, almost a premonition, that going back to Houston would be the biggest mistake of her error-prone life.

Chapter Eleven

They hadn't flown out of Missoula International Airport as Chrysie had expected but had boarded a small noncommercial jet at a private airport a little more than an hour from Aohkii. The ride was bumpy, though no one seemed to notice but her. She fought to keep down the toast and coffee she'd had for breakfast while Josh and the kids munched on fruit, cookies and soft drinks from the plane's food cooler.

Josh stopped and joked with the kids as he walked back from the front of the plane, where he'd been chatting with the middle-aged pilot and a copilot who looked almost old enough to shave.

He moved the small pillow from his seat and sat down beside Chrysie. "We'll be landing in about ten minutes."

"In a real airport?"

"It's real but not large enough to handle anything but private and cargo planes."

"But it is in New Orleans?"

"It is. Rachel and Logan are meeting us there."

"This seems somewhat surreal."

"Meeting my brother and sister-in-law?"

"No, my life. Flying around in a chartered jet. Running from killers on a snowmobile. Returning to Houston but afraid to be seen in public or even to go to my house."

Josh reached over and took her hand. "The surreal part has been the past three years. Now we're going to set things right and put a stop to your running. And who knows? One of us may visit your house."

"Tell me about Rachel," she said, trying to concentrate on something besides problems.

"Rachel's an attorney, but she takes on mostly pro bono cases now when she's not volunteering her help with cleanup and rebuilding efforts following Katrina."

"Did they lose their house to the hurricane?"

"No, their new house is on the lake, but they built it pretty much hurricane-proof. They only live on the top two levels."

"Did she work for a law firm before the hurricane?"

"She was a corporate attorney with one of the most prestigious firms in town before they got married. One of the senior partners got caught with his pants down, and I do mean that literally. He was also found guilty of being an accessory to murder."

"That sounds like quite a story."

"It is. You should ask her to tell you all about it one day."

"Hey, look, there's a lake, and I can see sailboats on it," Danny called from the window seat on the other side of the narrow aisle.

Chrysie raised the shade and peered out her window. The boats were in plain sight, which meant they were descending faster than she'd anticipated. "Is everyone buckled in?" she asked as she leaned over to check the girls, who were in the two seats right in front of her and Josh.

"I'm buckled," Jenny answered.

"And so are the other three," Josh assured her. "I checked before I sat down."

They cleared Lake Pontchartrain, then bounced along the runway a few yards before settling down into a smooth taxiing speed.

"I see Aunt Rachel," Danny yelled. He was peering out his window and waving like crazy.

"Keep the seat belts buckled until the plane comes to a full stop," Josh reminded them.

Chrysie took a deep breath. She hadn't left Jenny or Mandy with anyone except school personnel since she'd left Houston. Now she was about to turn them over to strangers who would fly away with them.

Suppose Rachel and Logan weren't the wonderful people Josh claimed. What if they were mean to the children or didn't watch them closely and let them get hurt? What if Mandy had nightmares? Would they know how to calm her? And Jenny's fever rose so quickly when she got a case of tonsillitis. Rachel didn't have children. What would she know about pediatric doses of medication?

But then, what kind of caretakers would the girls have if Chrysie went to jail for the rest of their childhood?

The plane stopped. The boys were out of their seat belts in a second. Josh stood and walked to the front of the plane. "Better make sure you have those electronic toys," he said. Danny and Davy got down on the floor for a thorough check. Davy came up with a small cartridge. "I almost left my best game."

Chrysie stretched to reach the small overhead compartment. "Don't bother with the luggage," Josh said. "We're going on to Houston in this plane after it refuels, and I'll get Logan to help me get the children's luggage."

Once the rolling stairs were in place, Josh opened the door and the boys pushed in front of him, hopping and jumping their way down the steps. Jenny followed behind Josh, then dropped back to stay close to Chrysie and Mandy.

The boys jumped from the bottom step and went tearing across the tarmac. A man who looked almost exactly like Josh lifted Danny and swung him around while a very attractive woman captured Davy in a bear hug. A second later the order was reversed, and all the while the boys were whooping it up as if it were the rodeo, Christmas and the Fourth of July all rolled in together.

This time the girls did not catch their excitement. Mandy kept a tight grip on Chrysie's hand, and Jenny clutched a handful of loose fabric on the leg of Chrysie's trousers.

The woman left the boys, who were bouncing around Logan and Josh, and headed Chrysie's way. She looked like a model in her tailored blue cashmere sweater and a pair of stylish gray trousers that showed off her long legs and shapely hips. Not a hair of her auburn bob was out of place.

She smiled and extended a perfectly manicured hand. "Rachel McCain, and you must be Chrysie."

"Yes, and this is Mandy and Jenny."

Rachel stooped and put herself at eye level with the girls. "I'm very pleased to meet you. I'm Davy and Danny's aunt Rachel."

"Do you make them eat all their peas?" Jenny asked.

"I'm afraid not. I don't like peas much myself. Danny likes broccoli, though, and Davy likes green beans, so I make sure to keep lots of those around. What do you like to eat?"

"I like peas," Mandy said, "and pancakes."

"Mmm. Pancakes. That's one my favorite breakfasts. What about you, Jenny?"

"I like ice cream."

"Me, too. I love strawberry."

"I like vanilla," Jenny said, finally letting go of Chrysie's trousers.

"I hope you like the beach," Rachel said. "That's where we're going on our vacation while your Mommy and Josh do some work."

"I wish my mom could come with us," Jenny said.

Chrysie laid a hand on Jenny's shoulder. "Next time, sweetie. Next vacation I'll be there with you." Unless she was in prison—or… No, she could not go there, could not let herself think she might not be reunited with the girls soon.

Mandy reached over and tugged on Rachel's hand to get her full attention. "What's a beach?"

"A beach is a marvelous place with lots of soft sand for digging and building castles and warm blue water for wading in."

Mandy clapped her hands, and Jenny managed a shy smile.

The woman was good with children. Chrysie should be grateful for that, and she was, but still she had that sinking feeling as if she were about to lose more than a few days with the girls.

Josh called to the girls to come and meet Logan. Mandy ran to him at once. Jenny looked to Chrysie first. "Don't leave yet, Mommy."

Chrysie swallowed past a huge lump. "No, sweetie. I won't leave yet."

"I can't even imagine how difficult this must be for you," Rachel said once the girls were out of hearing distance.

"I've never left them with strangers, not since their father was murdered."

"Josh told us a little of your situation. You must have been terrified yesterday when those men showed up at the ranch."

"I was. I still am."

"What's the news on Cougar this morning?" Rachel asked.

"He's still listed as critical, but the doctor says there's some improvement. They're hopeful for a full recovery."

"Good. I've only met him once, but he seemed like a really nice guy."

Chrysie only nodded. If they started talking about the danger and the murderous monsters, she'd never be able to leave the girls.

"We'll take good care of them," Rachel said as if reading her mind. "I won't let them out of my sight. And it won't just be me watching them. Logan's hired two bodyguards, retired Secret Service men. They're the best in the business and great at staying inconspicuous, so the children won't feel threatened by them."

"Where are you going?"

"To one of the McCain properties in the Cayman Islands. It's a small hotel, but one that caters to the very rich and to entertainers who like complete privacy. Logan chose it for its security."

"I appreciate this—more than you know."

"Logan would do anything for Josh and vice versa. They lost contact for years, but now they're as close as brothers can get. Besides, we're thrilled to spend time with Danny and Davy and we can both use a vacation."

Chrysie reached into the side pocket of her handbag and pulled out a small black notebook. "I made a list of things you might need to know about each of the girls. And I packed their vitamins and medications with directions, just in case they get sick. Neither of them has any allergies."

Rachel took the notebook and slipped it into her pocket. "Thanks. I'll look over all the notes on the flight. If I have any questions, I'll call you, and you can and check on Jenny and Mandy any time you like."

Rachel linked her arm with Chrysie's as they went to join the others. The four adults talked for a few minutes before Josh and Logan went back to the plane for the children's luggage. Minutes later it was time to say goodbye.

Chrysie's heart had never felt heavier, but she put on a good show for the girls' sakes, smiling and talking of how much fun they'd have. She gave them one last kiss and hug as they boarded the plane for the Cayman Islands, a small luxury jet with McCain Industries emblazoned on the side.

Josh put his arm around Chrysie's shoulders as the McCain jet taxied down the tarmac toward eventual takeoff. "They'll be safe," he said. "And so will you. Now let's get this show on the road. We've got a murder case to solve."

There was no doubt in his voice, no quiver of weakness or tremor of fear. That, as much as anything, helped her think positively as she tried to prepare herself mentally for Houston and the problems she'd tried to run away from for the past three years.

JOSH DROVE ACROSS Houston in a rented car that he had waiting for them when they landed. The traffic was horrendous, typical for a Houston weekday afternoon but totally different from the roads anywhere around Aohkii.

Traffic was the least of Chrysie's worries. Her emotions were on a new roller coaster. She dreaded dealing with the issues at hand, hated that they would be delving into the murder on a firsthand basis, knowing that danger could lurk behind every corner. Yet the familiarity of the skyline, the myriad Mexican restaurants, even the humidity seemed welcoming. This was home, and she'd missed it terribly, especially before she'd moved to Aohkii.

"We've gone one mile in the last twenty minutes," Josh complained. "How did you ever stand this traffic?"

"It's not always like this. There's probably a wreck."

"That's because they have about a million too many cars on the freeway. Give me Montana any day."

"I like the city."

"What's to like, unless you dig smog and people?"

"Museums, plays, shopping and concerts. And we have the Astros, the Rockets and the Texans. Anything you want, you can get in Houston."

"Good, let's start with records—Jonathan's, to be exact. What financial records did he keep at home?"

"Financial records?"

"Bank statements, phone bills—cellular and landline—credit cards."

The welcoming feeling vanished, leaving nothing but dread and the feeling that disaster was hovering over them like a Texas tornado. She forced her mind to travel back to the daily routine from her past.

"Jonathan paid the household bills at the office. I don't recall his keeping any of those records or receipts at home. And anything business-related would have definitely been stored at the office. I know the police went through everything at our house and his office the day after the murder. I don't know what they took."

"Did you leave all the bill paying and budgeting to Jonathan?"

"Yes, all except the utilities, groceries and whatever clothes or incidentals we needed for me or the girls. I paid for those from my salary."

"Did you ever see a copy of his pay stub?"

"Not that I remember, but I didn't worry about things like that. I trusted him. I know that sounds ludicrous now in light of what I know about his being unfaithful, but still it's true."

"So we have to find a way to get into his office and see if we can locate those records."

"You don't mean break in?"

"That's not my first choice."

"His office is on the tenth floor of a building with excellent security. We can't just walk in."

"Nothing is so secure it can't be breached by cops or professional criminals."

"We don't even know if the records still exist," she said. "Luisa Pellot probably had Jonathan's secretary throw everything away when she cleaned out his office, especially since I wasn't around to claim them."

A red pickup truck swerved in front of Josh just as he switched lanes to avoid getting dumped onto the I-10 East exit. A string of curse words rolled off Josh's tongue. "Sorry. But the guy was an idiot."

"You just don't like city driving."

"You got that right. Now back to business. I think you made a good point about the records being moved.

I'm thinking I should check with Jonathan's secretary before we take the risk of breaking into the office."

"You can't do that. Vanessa will call the cops the second you show up."

"I am a cop, Chrysie. Got a gun, a badge. Hell, I even watch *CSI* occasionally. I can talk the talk as good as the next guy."

"You're a sheriff in Montana, not Texas."

"I'll flash my ID so fast that—what was her name again?

"Vanessa Templar."

"So fast Vanessa Templar will never notice. I'll tell her this is part of the continuing investigation."

"And I guess I stay in the hotel while you're questioning her, because I sure can't show up at her house. Even with my hair color and style changed, I'm sure she'd recognize me."

"That's the other thing. We're not actually renting a hotel room. We're staying with a buddy of mine."

"And he knows I'm wanted for murder?"

"Wanted for questioning in a murder. That's a far different thing. And he doesn't know officially."

"What's the difference in knowing and knowing officially?"

"If he knew officially, he'd have to turn you in or risk losing his job."

Chrysie threw her hands up in the air, at least as far as she could throw them in the confines in the car.

"This just keeps getting worse and worse. First you tell me you're going to visit the woman who was having an affair with my husband. Then you tell me I'm staying with someone in law enforcement who knows but doesn't know I'm a fugitive from justice."

"Take it easy. Grecco and I were roomies in college before I flunked out. He's fine with this."

"Grecco? He sounds like some sort of heavy."

"This is no time for prejudice, sweetheart. Grecco is personable and he'll take good care of you. Besides, he's the one who found out that your late husband was not quite the law-abiding attorney you thought."

"What are you talking about?"

"It seems that your husband was under suspicion of selling Mexican babies on the black market after smuggling the pregnant illegal aliens and the rest of their families across the border."

Selling babies. The idea of it made her sick. The thought that Jonathan might have been involved in something so abhorrent was unfathomable. "When was he suspected of that?"

"Around three years ago, just before he joined up with Luisa Pellot."

Back when he'd fretted constantly that he couldn't get his career off the ground. "Where did you hear this?"

"From Grecco. He was with Border Patrol back then."

"And now?"

"Now's he's with Homeland Security but working on securing our borders."

"When did Grecco tell you this?"

"Yesterday, right before I tried to call Cougar and got no answer. You can see how it slipped my mind."

Acid pooled in her stomach. She didn't want to believe this about Jonathan. She shouldn't even be talking about it when he was no longer alive to defend himself.

Yet he'd given someone reason to kill him. She hated these doubts, but an icy dread was seeping into her bones, and her gut feeling was that there would be no good discoveries about Jonathan from here on out. Was it possible she could have lived with him for five years and known so little about him?

Yet here she was, trusting a man she barely knew with her life and his brother and sister-in-law, whom she didn't know at all, with her girls.

Memories from the last few days flashed through her mind. The way he joked to hide his emotions. The romantic side of him on a sleigh ride. Sitting across from Josh at the breakfast table. The look on his face when he'd pulled her into his arms yesterday after finding her and Mandy stranded in the snow. Making love with him.

She turned and studied his profile. She'd been attracted to him from the moment she'd first watched him stride onto the stage at the pageant rehearsal. Then it had been his rugged good looks and powerful charisma that had claimed her attention.

But there was so much more to the man. There was strength and determination and the way he did what was right no matter the cost. Like turning in drug dealers in New Orleans at the risk of his life. Like taking on all her problems when he could have just made a phone call and turned her in to the police.

She reached over and rested her hand on his thigh. "Thanks."

"What was that for?"

"For being here, for being you."

He put his hand over hers and squeezed it. "Baby, you ain't seen nothing yet."

VANESSA TEMPLAR LIVED in a frame-and-brick house in an older neighborhood on the northwest side of Houston, thankfully the same house she'd lived in when she'd worked for Jonathan Harwell. It made tracking her down so much easier.

There were weeds in the flower bed, and dead blossoms were interspersed liberally with bright yellow ones on the blooming mums. But there were still signs of the season. A faded plastic drummer boy guarded the wreath of fake poinsettias on the front door.

It was a quarter to six when Josh knocked on the door. An attractive woman, probably in her mid to late thirties, opened it just far enough to peer out. He could hear the TV blaring out a *Friends* rerun in the background.

"Can I help you?" she asked.

"I hope so," Josh said, keeping his tone professional but friendly. "I'm looking for Vanessa Templar."

"I'm Vanessa."

He pulled his ID card with the embossed badge from his back pocket and opened the leather holder, flashing his ID for a mere fraction of a second before slamming the holder shut again.

She clung to the knob but didn't open the door any wider. "What's this about?"

"You're not in any trouble," he assured her. "I just want to ask you a few questions."

She looked puzzled.

"I understand you used to work for Jonathan Harwell."

She opened the door a bit wider. "I was his secretary before he was murdered, but I told the police everything I knew three years ago."

"That's all on file," Josh said, "but I just need to clarify a few things. It won't take but a few minutes."

"You can come in, but I didn't know anything then and I still don't." She led him through the foyer and into a large family room that looked out over the backyard. He took a seat on one end of the sofa while she tossed a couple of pillows around and looked under a stack of magazines, finally coming up with the remote for the TV.

"Kids leave it on all the time," she said, "even when they're not watching it." She turned it off and tossed the remote to the coffee table.

"How many children do you have?"

"I only have one daughter, but my boyfriend's two boys are staying with us this week."

"Do you still work at the same law office? Let's see…that was Pellot and Harwell, wasn't it?"

"That was the name of the firm. It's just Luisa Pellot, Attorney at Law, now. But to answer your question, I'm not with the firm anymore. Luisa let me go about three months after Mr. Harwell was killed."

Vanessa straightened the magazines while she talked, then set them on the edge of the coffee table. "Can you excuse me just a second? I left some potatoes boiling and I need to check them."

"Sure. No problem." Josh watched her walk away. He couldn't see a man cheating on Chrysie for any other woman, but he could see a guy being attracted to Vanessa. Nice figure, and the jeans and sweater showed it off. Nice hair, too. Wavy, dark brown, shiny and long enough to fall halfway to her waist.

When she rejoined him, she perched on the armrest of the opposite end of the sofa, almost as if she were ready to make a quick getaway. "Are there any new leads on who might have killed Mr. Harwell?"

"I'm not at liberty to say," Josh said.

"I know that his wife was a suspect for a while, but I'm certain Dr. Harwell didn't do it."

"What makes you so sure?"

"She wasn't the type. She was quiet, but really smart. She gave me advice on raising Abby several times. Abby's my daughter. Actually, I could use some of Dr. Harwell's advice now. Abby turns thirteen next summer, and all she wants to do is hang out in those computer chat rooms. It worries me."

"It should. They can be very dangerous places."

Vanessa shook her head. "If you're here to ask about that affair I supposedly had with Mr. Harwell, the answer hasn't changed. I never had any inappropriate relations with him."

So that was her side of this. Josh had to assume she hadn't seen the picture of her and Jonathan in that hot and heavy embrace.

"I wonder how that rumor got started," he said, hoping Vanessa would say more on the subject.

"I have no idea, but I don't think it was by anyone in our office. Mr. Harwell was the perfect gentleman. He never flirted with the office staff."

Very interesting. And either Vanessa was a good— no, make that a great—liar or she and Jonathan had never been a thing. Which meant someone had gone to a lot of trouble to doctor that photograph and mail it to Chrysie.

"How did Mr. Harwell and Mrs. Pellot get along?" He knew Chrysie's opinion of that, but it would be nice to hear Vanessa's, as well.

"It's hard to say. Sometimes they laughed and talked like friends. Other times things seemed strained between them. I guess it was the partnership thing—you know, a little business rivalry."

"What do you mean by *strained?* Did they argue? Talk about the other person behind their back."

"Oh, no. Nothing like that. It was just, you know, we'd be having coffee in the office lounge and one might snap at the other." Vanessa smiled. "Usually it was Luisa who did the snapping. We women have those hormonal swings, you know."

Josh was not about to be drawn into the topic of women's hormones. Besides, it was time to get to the real point of his visit. "Do you recall what was done with Mr. Harwell's personal records that were filed in his office?"

"The police took some of the records, but mostly they took client files, in case one of them had a motive for murdering Mr. Harwell. At least that's why Luisa said they took them. She probably knows since her younger sister is a homicide detective with the Houston PD."

Boy, the treats just kept coming. He'd love to

know more about the sister in homicide, but he didn't dare ask. "What happened to the rest of Mr. Harwell's records?"

Vanessa pursed her lips, then grimaced. "I don't know if I should tell you this."

"Can't go wrong talking to the police."

"Well, Mrs. Pellot said I should shred all his files that weren't pertinent to the business, but I felt bad about doing that, so I took his private records to his house, just in case his wife came back. As far as I know, she never did."

"Then you must have had a key to the Harwells' house."

"No, but I have the code to open their garage door. I used to drop paperwork off for Mr. Harwell from time to time, and he'd just have me leave it in the garage, so that's what I did with the records."

Which is what Josh had come to hear, though he'd gotten a lot more information than he'd bargained for. He wrapped up the questioning and left, eager to drive back to Grecco's and fill Chrysie in on everything.

The woman got to him. Well, that was the understatement of the year. He was absolutely bewitched by her.

He didn't know where the relationship was going, but he had no intention of going back to Montana until she was cleared of all charges and the dirty dogs who'd shot Cougar and come after her were in jail.

He hoped it didn't take long. God, he hated this traffic.

JUAN HERNANDEZ started back to his office with a cup of stale but very hot coffee. It was never hot enough for him out of the pot, not even when it was freshly perked. He always nuked it for thirty seconds.

He took a sip. Perfect. The temperature of the coffee was the only thing right in his life today. Angela's door was open a few inches, which either meant the cleaning crew was already pushing the dirt around or Angela was still here.

He stopped. No vacuum noises. He rapped his knuckles on the door.

"Come in, unless you have a problem. I'm off duty."

He stuck his head inside the door. "So why are you still here?"

"Just finishing up this report. What's up? Did your prisoner finally show?"

"Assuming you're talking about Cassandra Harwell, the answer is no. And she wasn't on any plane that left Missoula, Montana, today, either, unless it was under an assumed name."

"Did you contact the clueless Montana sheriff who called you the other day?"

"I tried to reach him. It seems he's on vacation,

and no one knows when he'll be back. I also called the Montana state police to alert them that Cassandra might be in the area. They said no one had reported seeing her, but there had been an attempted murder in Aohkii yesterday. And—get this—the man was shot on Sheriff Josh McCain's ranch."

"Lots of excitement for a town that's not even on the map. Do you think Cassandra had something to do with the shooting?"

"I would not put anything past that murdering bitch."

"Don't make this about your daughter, Juan. If you do, it will just get you all messed up again."

Angela met his gaze and he looked away. He didn't need pity. "It's not about my daughter.

"Good. Keep me posted."

"Sure." He turned and went back to his office. It wasn't about his daughter. It was about Dr. Harwell's not getting away with murder—again.

ANGELA WAITED UNTIL Juan was in his office, then closed her door and punched in her sister's cell phone number.

"Luisa Pellot speaking."

"Have you got a minute?"

"Angela. Nice surprise. I didn't notice the call was from you—that's how busy I am. But I can spare a minute. What's up?"

"More news on Cassandra Harwell, and you are not going to believe this."

CHRYSIE GROANED WITH every bump—which she'd estimate at one a minute—a painful workout for her muscles which were still bruised and throbbing from the snowmobile excursion. Thankfully she didn't have to ride but a few blocks in the car's trunk. That was the concession she'd agreed to in exchange for going with him to examine Jonathan's records.

The car stopped, and her left knee slammed into the spare tire. The engine noise went silent. A second later she heard the slam of the car door, and her already ragged nerves strained to near breaking as the trunk flew open.

It had been three years since she'd left, but she was finally home. Hopefully her welcome would not be a warrant for her arrest.

Chapter Twelve

Chrysie took Josh's hand for support as she unwound herself from the fetal position and climbed out of the trunk. They were in the garage, overhead door down, and out of sight of anyone who might be watching the house.

"I don't see any boxes," Josh said. "Vanessa may have been a better liar than I took her for."

Chrysie stretched and scanned rows of shelves. Everything was just as it had been when she'd left. Her Navigator looked as if it hadn't been driven. The only thing that was missing was Jonathan's Acura, but that had been leased by the law firm.

"Maybe Marv found the records and carried them inside," she said. "Since you said he's taking care of everything, he must also check the house occasionally to be sure it's in good repair. He'd have to keep the lawn and flower beds up, as well. Otherwise the neighbors would have him in court and paying hefty fines for neglect of property. This is a very exclusive neighborhood."

"I noticed that driving in, but the good thing is the lush landscaping hides the house from the street. Someone would have to come halfway down the drive before they could tell that lights are on in the house."

She knew there was a good possibility that the police might do just that, but she and Josh had considered and planned for that possibility. She just had to trust that their plan would work.

Josh tried the door to the house, but it was locked tight. Chrysie handed him the key that she'd taken with her the night she'd run. "The locks may have been changed."

"Not likely since the garage code you gave me worked."

She took a deep breath as Josh fit the key into the lock. "Ready or not, here I come."

A second later she was standing inside the mudroom. The neon lights flickered at the touch of the switch, then steadied, bathing the high-ceilinged rectangular space and making the white floor tiles gleam. She paused in front of the mahogany bench. Jonathan's boots were sitting beneath it, neatly waiting as if he would return momentarily.

This had been her world, yet it seemed almost

foreign to her now. Three years of the nomadic life had changed her.

The room grew suddenly brighter, and the surprise paralyzed her with fear. Someone had turned on the kitchen light.

Josh pulled his gun. "Stay back," he whispered as he walked ahead. "Police," he called. "Who's there?"

There was no answer. She stepped into the kitchen and scanned the area. Josh was nowhere in sight. She took one of the carving knives from the drawer nearest the range and held it front of her.

"You can drop the knife," Josh said as he joined her in the kitchen. "No one's here but us. Evidently some of the lights in the house are programmed to go on and off automatically. Looks as if the attorney who's managing your estate is on the ball."

"When I see Marv, I'll be sure to thank him for nearly giving me a heart attack."

"Good timing, though," Josh said. "I'm sure the cops who patrol the neighborhood know the schedule, so they won't think anything about the lights being on while we work."

She returned the knife to the drawer. "Then let's work fast before they go off again."

"You got it." Josh scanned the kitchen and gave a low whistle. "This is a fancy spot for cooking grits."

Interesting comment considering it hadn't been designed for cooking anything. It was a pretentious show kitchen, the same as the rest of the house had been. "The house was Jonathan's statement that we'd arrived."

It occurred to her how foreign that concept would sound to Josh. He'd been born with the silver spoon in his mouth and had spit it out to become his own man. He was comfortable with chartered jets and money to pay for bodyguards, but if they hadn't been readily available, she was certain he'd have still found a way to get the job done.

She relaxed a little, thankful that that her nerves hadn't become totally unglued by walking into the house. And then she stepped into the wide hallway and looked up at the winding staircase and the spot where Jonathan's killer had been standing when he'd dangled Mandy over the banister. Her composure dissolved, and she stood there, frozen to the spot as her knees buckled and the walls closed in on her.

Josh caught her before she fell. "It's okay, baby. I'm right here."

She held on to him until she regained her equilibrium. She'd get through this. She had to. But she wasn't ready to handle the staircase or the master bedroom just yet. "The room Jonathan used for his home office is just down the hall," she said. "Maybe the boxes of records are there."

She led the way, not looking to the left or right,

determined to think positively and not to let the house and the terrifying memories get to her like that again.

The French doors to Jonathan's office were open. His desk and bookshelves were as neat as ever, but the floor was cluttered with packing boxes.

"Those must be the records," she said.

Josh high-fived her, clearly excited at the daunting task that lay ahead. "Looks as if Vanessa was telling the truth."

"At least about the boxes," Chrysie said. "So where do we start?"

"I'll rip into a few," Josh said, "and see which have the most potential."

Seconds later they were both in the middle of the floor surrounded by redundant records that as far as Chrysie could tell had absolutely no bearing on Jonathan's murder.

Her heart fell. This was probably their final dead end. Two hours later, she was more convinced of that than ever.

"WHO WAS THAT on the phone?"

Vanessa replaced the receiver, then dropped onto the sofa next to her boyfriend. "It was one of my ex-employers."

"Which one?" Chad rested his glass of iced tea on a Texas-star coaster that decorated the coffee table.

"Luisa Pellot. I told you about her."

"Oh, yeah. Her partner got murdered by his wife. What was his name? Jonathan Hostel?"

"Harwell. And it was only speculation that his wife killed him. I never believed it. She wasn't that kind of person. Anyway that was three years ago, yet that's the second person today who's contacted me about the Harwells."

"Who else called you?"

"A cop, only he didn't call. He stopped by the house this afternoon to ask questions about Mr. Harwell. And Mrs. Pellot was calling to say that if I happened to hear from Mrs. Harwell, I should call her at once, said she had information she thought Cassandra Harwell would want."

"I thought Mrs. Harwell was on the lam."

"She was, but for some reason Mrs. Pellot thinks she may be returning to Houston."

"That's trouble you don't need, sweetheart. Don't even answer the phone if that Harwell woman calls you."

Vanessa started to mention the fact that the police had all but accused her of having an affair with Mr. Harwell before he was killed, but decided against it. Chad was jealous enough of her current boss without giving him a dead one to worry about.

Still, two incidents in one day—something was definitely up.

AN HOUR LATER and still no closer to finding whatever Josh had hoped for, Chrysie took a break. She stretched out on the carpet, using a stack of outdated credit card statements for a pillow. In spite of their bad luck, she was thrilled that Logan had called to let her tell the girls good-night.

They'd seemed fine without her. She was relieved but feeling just a tad displaced. Her mind drifted back to the things Josh had told her about his visit with Vanessa. "Why do you think Vanessa is still so adamant she didn't have an affair with Jonathan when the evidence was so convincing?"

"She may not have seen the photograph."

"I just assumed the police would have shown it to her."

"We law enforcement personnel have a way of only giving out information when it suits our purpose. Besides, it's possible that she didn't have an affair with him."

"Pictures don't lie."

"Sure they do. Someone skilled with the use of a good photo software program could have put Jonathan's face on the picture of a baboon and made it look natural."

"But why go to all that trouble just to make me think he was unfaithful if he wasn't? Unless…" The ugly information from Grecco crept back into her mind. "I still can't believe Jonathan was involved in selling babies on the black market, but if he was, I suppose someone he stole a baby from might have sent the picture to get back at him."

"Could be." Josh pulled a new stack of envelopes from the box. "But more likely the photograph was part of the setup to give you a motive."

"If every man who was having an affair got killed by his wife, there would be an extreme shortage of men on this planet."

Josh only nodded and pulled another stack of envelopes from the box he was currently inspecting.

"Your theory is flawed," she said.

"How's that?"

"The picture was sent to me, and if I hadn't made the mistake of leaving it lying around, the police would never have seen it. So how would that have helped set me up?"

"The anonymous photographer may have sent the police a copy, as well, after the fact, so that it looked as if they were just trying to help in the investigation." Josh held up what looked like a bank deposit slip. "Now this is interesting."

Chrysie sat up and scooted closer to Josh to see what he was scrutinizing. "I never knew Jonathan had an account with that bank. It's not where we had our savings or our checking accounts."

"This account only has Jonathan's name on it."

She took the deposit slip from his hand. It showed

a five-hundred-thousand-dollar cash deposit made in March of the same year he'd signed on with Luisa Pellot, one month before their official merger.

"Here's another cash deposit Jonathan made for the same amount."

Chrysie's stomach pitched and rolled. Deposits like that gave Grecco's allegations a lot more substance. Only she couldn't—or wouldn't—believe she'd been married to a man involved in something as abhorrently perverted as selling babies.

"Here's a statement that shows another large deposit. That money had to be coming from somewhere."

"He could have been stealing from our joint accounts."

"I've checked those. There were no large cash withdrawals. And his pay from the firm was electronically deposited into the joint accounts, so there would be no slips like these for those."

"I don't know where he was getting the money," Chrysie said, "but it explains how we could afford this pretentious house and all the expensive furnishings."

"This account was active the last two years of his life," Josh said. "The deposits were made roughly every six months. That would have made the next one due the day after his murder."

"What are you getting at?"

"Regular cash payments in large amounts with no explanation as to the source of the funds. A secret bank account. I hate to say it, Chrysie, but this has all the earmarks of blackmail."

She stretched her legs in front of her, then pulled her knees to her chin. "If Jonathan was blackmailing someone, that would definitely give them a motive for killing him, especially with another payment due."

"That's one theory."

"If that's the case, then the two men who killed him and shot Cougar must be the ones Jonathan was blackmailing."

"Not necessarily. They may have been hired by the person who was being blackmailed."

"You mean like paid assassins?"

"That's not nearly as uncommon as you'd think, Chrysie. Sick but not uncommon."

"But why didn't the Houston detectives look for any of this?"

"Because the evidence was stacked against you— and you ran. Not that I'm making excuses for them, but flight always makes a person look guilty."

Josh placed the bank statements back inside the box. "I want to take some of these records with us, but we should probably go back to Grecco's and sleep on this while I decide what to do next."

"You should go back to Aohkii while you're still alive," Chrysie said. "I'll go the police with what we have. They'll surely come to the same conclusion you did."

He kissed her, and the synergy they shared was deliciously reassuring. "We'll go to the police when it's time, but not before. I don't trust anyone to protect you but me."

And so they would go back to Grecco's and sleep on this. Right or wrong, she couldn't wait to climb under the sheets with him again and curl up in his arms.

She helped him carry the boxes to the car, leaving the last couple for him to get while she washed and put away the glasses. She was about to dry the first one when she heard the front door creak open followed by the click of high heels in the foyer.

She and Josh were no longer alone.

JOSH REACHED the central hallway just as a tall brunette carrying a huge bouquet of exotic flowers stepped through the front door. He set the box he was carrying on the steps and readied his hand to go for his gun.

The woman froze when she saw him.

"I'm Josh," he said, rushing with the introductions before she started screaming and throwing flowers at him. "I'm a private investigator working to gather evidence in the Jonathan Harwell murder case."

"I didn't expect anyone to be here."

"And I had no idea FTD delivered this time of night," he joked, talking loudly so that Chrysie would be certain to hear and have time to follow their plan to hide at the first sign of company.

"I'm Luisa Pellot," she said. "You may have heard of me. Jonathan Harwell and I were partners in a law firm."

The woman could have been anywhere from fifty to sixty, maybe older if her cosmetic surgeon was good enough. Judging from the sophisticated black dress and the diamond necklace, she was returning from some sort of social function.

Suspicion tugged at the corners of her mouth. "I know Marv Evinu has power of attorney over the Hartwell estate. Did he hire you?"

"He did."

That seemed to ease her mind a little or at least eased the furrows in her brow. "Well, I hope you're coming up with something to clear Cassandra. She's a dear, you know. A good mother, sweet as can be. We all told the police that, but they just zeroed in on her as a suspect. I don't think they ever looked anywhere else."

"I'm sure she'd appreciate your vote of confidence. So why the flowers?"

She smiled sheepishly. "I can't say where I heard it, but there's a rumor that Cassandra is coming back to Houston. If she does return, I thought the flowers would be a nice touch, something to make her feel as if she was really coming home."

"That's thoughtful." It didn't take a lot of imagination to figure out that she'd heard the rumor from her detective sister. But apparently Luisa hadn't gotten the message that Chrysie would be arrested as soon as she showed her face.

"I'll just put these in some water," Luisa said.

Josh followed her into the kitchen. Thankfully Chrysie was nowhere in sight. He didn't see Luisa as a threat, but he didn't want her running to her sister with news that Chrysie was in town.

Luisa opened cabinets until she found a vase that suited her. "I only live a few blocks from here, so I drive by here often. That's why Marv gave me a key. He said if I was going to check on the outside, I may as well do him a favor and check on the inside, as well." Luisa worked on the arrangement as she talked, then stood back to admire her handiwork.

"They look good," Josh said. "I hope someone besides me shows up to appreciate them, since I'm on my way out."

"I hope Cassandra shows up. I really need to talk to her."

"What about?"

"I know she heard some things about Jonathan that upset her. I think I could clear that up for her and relieve her mind."

"If you want to tell me, I can try to get the information to her."

"No, it's personal. It can wait until I see her. But I'll be glad to help with your investigation any way I can." She reached into the small black sequined bag that had hung from her wrist and took out a business card. "You can reach me at the office tomorrow after noon or at my house before that," she said, handing him the card.

"I may just show up."

"Good. Now what did say your name was again?"

He'd figured that was coming. "Josh Morgan," he said, going back to the alias he'd used when he'd first moved to Montana. "Sorry, I don't have a business card with me."

She nodded. "That's okay. Marv wouldn't hire anyone but the best. He's an excellent attorney, and he and Jonathan were good friends."

He walked her to the door. "Don't be surprised if I show up at the law firm tomorrow afternoon."

"I'll be anticipating that with pleasure."

Josh closed and locked the door behind Luisa, then picked up the box he'd left on the stairs and headed for the garage. He didn't have Luisa Pellot figured out, but she seemed pretty much as Chrysie had described her—good-natured, a little nosy, liked to talk.

He suspected she'd come by tonight just to see if there were any sign that Chrysie had been there. The only sign had been the two glasses on the counter, and if they had registered with her at all, she'd given no indication.

Chrysie was waiting in the garage. In less than five minutes she was back in the trunk and they were on their way. The blackmail angle was promising, but he'd have to know all the players before he went to the police.

He couldn't bear to think of Chrysie being locked in a jail cell for even a day. He pretty much didn't want her anywhere except with him—in Montana. Houston was okay for a day or two, but it was no place to live. Even a hardheaded Texan woman had to know that.

SEAN ROGERS HUNG UP the phone. "Damn bitch. Can't please her. For two cents, I'd take her out. She acts like she don't think I could."

"It's not our fault we lost our tail on the Harwell woman. They had a friggin' blizzard up there. Did you tell her that?"

"Can't tell her anything. Anyway, after she chewed me out, she said not to worry, that everything was taken care of. Said the alternative plan would be just as effective."

"What the hell does that mean?"

"I don't know." Sean poured another shot of tequila from the bottle they'd picked up at the liquor store on the way in from the airport. "I told her we hung out at the airport in Missoula as long as we dared considering half the cops in Montana were looking for us for shooting that guy at the sheriff's ranch."

Mac headed to the bathroom. "Boss lady should have let us finish off the shrink that night we killed her old man."

"Woulda, coulda, shoulda. It's all water under the bridge now."

Sean finished the shot and poured another. A little lime would be good about now, but they forgot to buy any. He kicked off his shoes and fell onto the lumpy mattress. He'd be glad to get back to Brownsville and his own bed.

His thoughts were interrupted by a knock. It was about time their pizza arrived. He padded over in his stocking feet and yanked the door open.

The delivery went straight through his heart.

JOSH'S EYES WERE CLOSED when Chrysie finished her shower and joined him in the guest bedroom at Grecco's town house. As badly as she needed his touch, she tried not to wake him as she slid between the crisp cotton sheets, but he reached for her before her head touched the pillow.

"I didn't mean to wake you."

"You didn't," he said. "I was just thinking." He pulled her close and kissed her, then trailed his right hand down her naked body and back up again, stopping to fondle one breast and then the other.

"Tell me about your life in Houston," he said. "Not the bad, just the ordinary things. Did you have friends? Did you like your work? What did you do on Saturday nights and lazy Sunday afternoons?"

"Why the sudden interest?"

"It hit me when I walked into your house tonight how little I know about you. You are a very complex woman."

"I'm no more complex than you, Josh."

"I'm just a cowboy sheriff running a ranch and raising my sons."

"And rescuing damsels in distress."

He kissed her and she melted into it, loving the taste of him and the mingling of their breaths. She wanted more, so much more, but she wasn't quite ready to let the conversation go.

"Tell me about Danny and Davy, Josh. How is it that they weren't part of your life until they were four years old?"

"It's not the best of bedtime stories."

"I'd still like to hear it."

He stiffened and pulled away from her.

"It's okay," she said, not wanting to upset him. "We can save it for another night."

"No real reason to wait. If you can stand to hear my faults, I guess I can throw them out there so you can get a glimpse of the real me."

Chapter Thirteen

Josh rolled out of bed and walked to the window. He'd never told anyone about the boys' early life. He'd always believed his hesitancy to discuss it was because he hoped Danny and Davy never had to deal with it. But he realized tonight that wasn't the whole story.

He didn't want to deal with it. He'd made a lot of mistakes when he was in his late twenties and very early thirties. Back then, he'd blamed all his weaknesses on his father. That had been a cop-out. The responsibility for his actions lay with no one but himself.

He'd tried to convince himself that he'd made everything right when he'd helped take the worst of the drug dealers off the streets of New Orleans, but that hadn't begun to make up for his sins of omission where his sons were concerned.

He'd had unprotected sex with a young woman he barely knew, and as a result, Danny and Davy had spent the first four years of their lives in a morally depraved environment and almost paid for his irresponsibility with their lives.

He exhaled slowly, blowing out a stream of hot breath and frustration. "I don't know where to start."

Chrysie propped herself up on one elbow. "Did you love the boys' mother?"

"I hate to say this, but I barely remember her. Tess was a one-night stand on an evening I'd had too much to drink." The muscles tightened in his stomach. "I had no idea that our sexual relations had resulted in her becoming pregnant with twins."

"When did she tell you?"

"Never. Apparently we hadn't even exchanged names. Eventually she saw a picture of my brother on the society pages of the *Times-Picayune* and mistook him for me. In her mind, Logan McCain was the biological father of her twins."

"Did she go to Logan?"

"No, she feared that if he knew about the boys, he'd use his money and influence to get custody of them—at least that's what she told Rachel."

"What kind of work did she do?"

Josh paced. "Tess worked for the Fruits of Passion, a gentlemen's club in the New Orleans French Quarter. She claimed she was an exotic dancer, but she did a lot more than dance."

"Like hustle?"

"Even more than that. She was involved in some

extremely perverted sexual activities the club provided for some of the city's richest and most prominent men."

"How had Logan learned about the boys if she didn't tell him?"

"One of the dancers who worked with Tess had sense enough to realize the boys were in danger. She sent Logan an anonymous note. He had their DNA tested and found out they were indeed McCains. He knew they weren't his, which meant they had to be mine."

"And this is when he still thought you were dead?"

"Right. Tess made a visit to Rachel at the law firm where she worked and told her that Logan McCain—who Rachel barely knew at that time—had impregnated her and was going to steal her children away from her just because he could. The next day Rachel discovered that Tess had been murdered."

"Did Rachel believe Logan had killed her?"

"At first." Josh stopped pacing and took a seat on the edge of the bed. "So did the cops. But by that time Danny and Davy were missing, and Logan was desperate to find them. Rachel got involved for the boys' sake and nearly got killed, as well."

"That must have gotten their relationship off to a rocky start."

"You'd think, but they not only fell in love but rescued Danny and Davy from the man who'd killed their mother and who planned to do the same with them after he collected a ransom from Logan."

Chrysie scooted across the bed, climbed onto her knees and started massaging the strained muscles in Josh's neck and shoulders. "No wonder you took a chance on me," she said. "You'd gone through some of the same type of trauma yourself—or at least Logan had on your behalf."

"Fortunately I was able to help a little. One of the cops who I'd worked with in setting up the drug sting let me know what was going on, and I made it back to New Orleans just in time to assist Logan in the boys' rescue."

"I'm quite sure you're underplaying your role in that."

"No, Logan and Rachel were the real heroes of that situation. I owe the boys' lives to them."

"What happened to the man who killed Tess?"

"He went to jail, along with several other men who were involved in the club's murderous perversions, including Rachel's boss. There's more, but the moral of the story is that I failed the boys when they were young. Now I'm doing my best to make it up to them and see that they have the kind of happiness they deserve."

It was over. He'd said it all, and it hadn't been nearly as hard as he'd feared. Credit Chrysie with that. She was far easier to talk to than any woman he'd ever met.

"I'm not too hot in the discipline department," he said, "but with the help of the right child psychologist, I could probably improve."

Chrysie wrapped her arms around his neck. "You're a super dad, Josh, and I understand exactly how you feel about the boys. It's the same for me. I'd give my life for my girls in a heartbeat."

Josh turned so that he could look her straight in the eye. "No more talk of giving your life. I mean it, Chrysie. I don't even want to hear you say that."

She snuggled against him and pressed her lips to his. The kiss took his breath away and awakened a swirling rush of need that he had no interest in fighting. They fell back onto the bed together, wrapped in a tangle of arms and legs and a hunger that took over his body and soul.

Like it or not, she was part of him now. And he was not about to lose her to a killer.

CHRYSIE POURED HER first cup of coffee of the morning and watched a few minutes of the local morning news on Grecco's small under-the-counter TV before joining Josh and Grecco at the kitchen table. Both men had their laptops out, but they were poring over the same bank statements and deposit slips Josh had scrutinized at her house last night.

She took the chair next to Josh's. "Any new thoughts on the subject now that you've slept on it?"

"Not really." He looked up from the paperwork. "You sound hoarse. Are you sure you feel okay?"

"It's just my sinuses." She looked at Josh's computer screen. It held what appeared to be a listing of dates and data from Jonathan's bank accounts. "So the two of you have had your heads together all morning and haven't come up with any new theories?"

Both shook their heads, but the look they exchanged made her very suspicious. She was about to question them further when her thoughts were interrupted by the young female broadcaster announcing a late-breaking news bulletin.

Grecco grabbed the remote and turned up the television's volume.

"Two men were found shot to death early this morning in a southeast Houston motel room after other guests reported hearing gunfire. The men have been identified as Mac Buckley and Sean Rogers, both residents of Brownsville, Texas. Police have released no further information on the double murder."

"Damn," Grecco muttered. "That screws my investigation to hell and back."

Josh stood and went to get a refill of coffee. "I take it you know the victims."

"They're the black-market baby suspects I was talking about earlier." Grecco pulled his laptop in front of him and punched a few keys. "Here's their pictures. Ugly sons of bitches, aren't they?" He pushed the computer to Chrysie so she could have a look.

Her heart jumped to her throat. "That's them! The ones who killed Jonathan."

Josh was at her side in an instant. "You're sure?"

"I'm positive. It all adds up with what you said last night. If Jonathan was killed by men involved in the baby ring, then he must have been blackmailing them. It explains the deposits and his murder."

Grecco pushed away from the table. "Looks like you may have nailed it, Josh. Now, if you two will excuse me, I've got to make a couple of very urgent phone calls."

Chrysie's pulse skyrocketed and relief crashed through her like a tidal wave. She stood and grabbed Josh's hands to anchor herself to reality as much as anything else.

"It's over," she said, finding it hard to believe. "All the fear. All the running. It's just over."

"Not quite," Josh said. "There's still the matter of a police investigation."

"But I can tell the police the full truth now. Once they realize what I was up against, they'll understand why I ran. I'll go in and talk to Detective Hernandez this morning. I am so ready to go on with my life."

"Not a good idea. You should let me do the talking

for you. It's always best to feel them out first and get our bargaining chips on the table."

"Do we have bargaining chips?"

"Yes, Dr. Harwell, I believe that we do."

She wasn't exactly sure what he meant by that, but she'd figure it out later. Right now she only wanted to revel in the knowledge that the men who'd haunted her every nightmare for the past three years were dead and her daughters were safe at last.

"Handle it however you want, Sheriff McCain, but right now I need a kiss."

Josh handled her request to perfection.

CHRYSIE HATED BEING left at Grecco's town house while Josh went to visit the HPD and Grecco rushed off to deal with the hoopla and complications involving his dead suspects. She was still so excited she could barely keep from going up on the rooftop and shouting the news to everyone who passed. She felt so free and…young.

Young. That was the operative word here. She felt as energetic and impetuous as a teenager and just as ready to jump into life. She'd love to go down to the clinic and share her great news with her colleagues, love to go shopping at the Galleria and buy dozens of presents for the girls, huge presents that didn't have to fit inside her old luggage so that they could be hauled from town to town.

A kitchen set and a bed for Mandy's doll. A bike for Jenny. And a puppy. This was going to be one terrific Christmas.

Only she couldn't go shopping or to the clinic just yet. She'd promised to stay at the condo until she heard from Josh. But she could at least go outside. She wouldn't even need a jacket. It was a balmy eighty-two degrees in Houston. Coming home had been the right thing to do after all.

Chrysie pocketed her cell phone and a few dollars just in case she came across a vending machine. There was not one diet soda in Grecco's fridge. How did men live on milk and beer alone?

The complex was bigger than she'd realized, and the location was terrific for a city dweller. There was a Mexican restaurant on the corner and a gourmet coffee shop across the street, the two staples of Houston life.

Chrysie took the stone path that led to the center of the complex and a lavishly landscaped swimming pool. It was hard to believe she'd gone from a freezing and very frightening snowmobile ride to this in a matter of two days.

She slipped out of her sneakers and dipped one big toe into the water. It was amazingly warm. In fact, too inviting to resist. So she rolled up her pants legs, took a seat on the edge of the pool and dangled her legs in the clear blue water.

She hadn't felt so safe and free in years, except that as soon as she started to totally relax, her mind drifted back to the sordid tale Josh had told her about his sons' mother.

One day Chrysie would face that same kind of situation with Mandy and Jenny. Eventually they'd ask about their father, and she'd have to tell them that Jonathan had been murdered because of his involvement with blackmail and the likes of Mac Buckley and Sean Rogers.

She only hoped that when all the facts were in they'd discover that he wasn't quite as morally corrupt as he appeared now. Which made her wonder what Luisa had been referring to last night when she'd told Josh that she had new information about Jonathan.

Josh had been too intrigued with the blackmail angle to give Luisa's comment much attention, but that didn't mean it wasn't important. Chrysie couldn't go to Luisa's home or office, as she'd suggested, but there was no reason she couldn't call her.

Josh had taken Luisa's business card with him this morning, but he'd left it on the dressing table last night with everything else from his pockets, and Chrysie had made a mental note of the number. The area code and prefix were the same as her cell number had been when she'd lived in Houston. And the last four numbers were 3399. Who could forget that?

She pulled her feet from the water and found a lounge chair in the shade before punching in the number. Luisa answered on the second ring.

Chrysie hesitated. This would be the first person she'd talked to from her old life. But the fear was finally over. It was time to move on.

"Hello, Luisa. This is Cassandra Harwell."

"Cassandra, what a delightful surprise."

Cassandra. The name made her feel like an imposter. Somewhere along the way she'd become a different person, and Chrysie fit her much better than her former name. She might just keep it.

"It's good to talk to you, too, Luisa."

"I've been worried sick about you and the girls. Are Mandy and Jenny okay?"

"They're fine."

"Tell me you're in town. I have so much to tell you."

"You can tell me on the phone."

The pause seemed to last forever. "I'd rather talk to you in person. And, actually, I know you're in town, Cassandra. I heard a rumor that your were returning and I saw the two freshly washed glasses on the counter at your house last night.

Chrysie saw no real reason to argue the issue when everyone would know soon. She'd either be in custody of the police while they finished the investigation or she'd be a free woman. Either way, she was through running.

"Perhaps we can get together tomorrow," Chrysie said.

"I'm leaving for the west coast this afternoon and I won't be back until after the Christmas holidays. I really don't think we should wait that long to talk. Can't we at least meet for coffee?"

A simple enough request if Chrysie hadn't promised Josh she wouldn't leave the complex. But then, just walking across the street wasn't actually leaving the complex. "How about meeting at a coffee shop in the Montrose area?"

"That would be ideal," Luisa said. "Just give me an address and about twenty minutes to get there."

Chrysie didn't know the address, but she gave Luisa directions.

"I know exactly where that is. I'll tell you what—if you get there first, order me a plain coffee and meet me on their side patio. We'll have more privacy that way. And I can promise you that what I have to tell will come as a complete surprise."

LUISA FLEW OUT OF her house five minutes later, briefcase in hand. She was halfway out of the garage when she noticed that the door that led from the back of her garage to the side garden was ajar. She was about to stop and close it, then realized that Manuel would have left it open. He was probably already weeding away at his chores.

She reached over and patted the briefcase again, assuring herself that she had what she needed. She hadn't lied. Cassandra would indeed be surprised.

CHRYSIE TRIED TO CALL Josh but got a busy signal. She could just leave a message, but she really wanted to talk to him and hear how things were going with the HPD. She'd call him back when she got to the coffee shop.

Chrysie had taken time to change into a clean pair of jeans and a plain white shirt. She felt a little underdressed even for coffee. Luisa was always dressed as if she were about to be photographed for a fashion magazine.

Luisa was waiting for her at one of the outside umbrella-covered tables. She looked right past Chrysie as she approached, obviously not recognizing her as a blonde.

Chrysie stopped at the table. "Hello, Luisa. It's been a while."

Luisa pulled off her sunglasses. "Cassandra?"

"One and the same."

"Wow! You look fabulous!"

"Thanks. You look great, too, as always."

Luisa stood and kissed Chrysie's cheek, lightly so as not to muss her lipstick.

"I took the liberty of ordering iced lattes for both of us," she said, pointing at two condensation-soaked glasses in front of her. "It's quite warm today, and I thought the cold drinks would be more refreshing."

"I agree." Chrysie took a sip of the coffee. It had a tangy sweetness she hadn't expected. "What's the flavor?"

"Toffee-nut. The signboard said it was their flavor of the day, and the girl behind the counter recommended it. If you don't like it, we can send yours back and you can choose something else."

"No, it's fine, just different."

They tried to make small talk while they drank their lattes, but the attempt fell flat. Their relationship had always been based on Jonathan's partnership with Luisa, and with that off the table, there was really nothing left.

About halfway through the coffee Chrysie found it difficult to even concentrate on what Luisa was saying. In fact, she was feeling a bit woozy, and the sun's glare seemed almost blinding. Worse, her throat was feeling drier by the second.

She took a big gulp of the drink. "I have to get back," she lied, "so what is it you wanted to tell me?"

"I have a photograph that's truly worth a thousand words. Walk over to the car with me and I'll show it to you."

She had trouble following what Luisa was saying. Maybe it was the drastic difference in climate between Montana and Houston that was making her feel so groggy. Or it could be those cold pills she'd taken this morning. She'd love to just put her head on the table and take a nap, but the sun was so bright.

Luisa hovered over her, tugging her arm. "Come with me, dear. This will only take a minute, and then I think I'd best drive you home. You're starting to look quite flushed."

Chrysie's feet dragged along the pavement until she found herself leaning against a black sedan. Luisa opened the back door of the car. "Get in, Cassandra. People are starting to stare. You don't want them to see you drunk in public."

"No, I'm not drunk. It's just…"

"Get in so that I can show you the picture."

"No." Chrysie tried to push away from the car but fell forward instead. Things were really fuzzy now, and Luisa's head seemed to be floating in space.

"Josh said…"

She didn't remember what Josh had said. She should call him. Only when she tried to take her phone from her pocket, her fingers just slid over it. She'd call him later. She had to lie down now. She fell to the seat of the car.

The car door slammed shut. She closed her eyes. She was cold and incredibly tired. She'd have to call Josh later.

Chapter Fourteen

Josh had gotten the runaround all morning from Juan Hernandez, and he was about to tell the detective what he could do with his threats and blustering when Hernandez finally agreed to bring his partner and his supervisor into the discussion.

The meeting was in the supervisor's office, a room three times the size of Hernandez's crowded space, with chairs that weren't piled with overflowing files. Hernandez had excused himself to go nuke a cup of stale coffee while they waited for his partner, Angela Martina, to finish a phone call.

Angela arrived before Hernandez returned. Josh had the fleeting sensation that he'd met her before, but he couldn't imagine where that might have been. After the introductions, she walked over to a handsomely framed magazine-size photograph of a boy and a dog that hung over the file cabinet.

"My wife loves the picture," the supervisor said.

"She wants to know when you're going to take one of my son and his dog."

"Anytime. But you should get my stepsister to photograph them. Luisa's the expert, especially at merging images the way I did with the girl and the cat. I'm still in the learning stages."

A female homicide detective with a stepsister named Luisa—had to be Luisa Pellot. No wonder Angela looked familiar. But they were stepsisters, not sisters, which could explain the vast age difference between the two.

And Luisa was an expert at merging images—like putting Jonathan's and Vanessa's faces on other people's bodies. That definitely added credence to his and Grecco's theory that she could have been the one Jonathan was blackmailing.

But still they lacked any real evidence. If Luisa Pellot had ever had anything to do with the baby black market or paid killers, she'd covered her tracks very well.

That could all change very soon. Grecco was on the situation like ketchup on fries, and he had the authority and technical equipment to take care of business.

Hernandez finally joined them, and Josh laid his cards on the table. He presented his findings, including the information Grecco had provided on this morning's motel victims. Bottom line, there was considerable evidence to indicate that while Cassandra Harwell may have run, she was not guilty of killing her husband.

Josh's cell phone rang just as he finished his spiel. The caller ID gave Chrysie's number. "Excuse me," he said, "but I have to take this."

He stepped into the hall. "What's up?"

Her response was muffled, as if she were a long way from the handset. "Speak up, Chrysie. I can't understand you." He could hear talking, but the reception was poor.

He walked a few yards down the hall and did the standard can-you-hear-me-now routine. Still indistinct. "We have a bad signal," he said. "I'll hang up and you call me back."

The response was still indistinguishable, but he'd almost swear he'd heard the word *blackmail*.

"Chrysie! Chrysie! Are you there?"

If she was, she wasn't talking. A cold dread knotted in his chest. He shouldn't have left her alone.

He kept the phone to his ear as he ran to the car without bothering to tell Hernandez he was out of there. He didn't hear anything else until he reached the pavement in front of police headquarters. The connection was only slightly clearer, but this time he was dead certain that the stifled voice had said *die*— and the voice did not belong to Chrysie.

CHRYSIE OPENED HER eyes and then closed them again when a stabbing pain struck at both temples. "Josh?"

"He's not here. You can never depend on men. You should know that by now."

The female voice rolled through the fog in Chrysie's head. "Luisa?"

"Yes, it's me. Don't worry. I have things under control. I hate that it has to be this way, but you really should have left Jonathan when you had the chance, Cassandra. The man was beneath you. And he was exceedingly greedy."

Chrysie shook her head gingerly, trying to clear away the fog. Images swam in and out as if they were fish in a murky pool. Luisa. The coffee shop. Something about a picture.

She tried to put her fingers to her aching head, but her hands wouldn't move. She closed her eyes and drifted back into the ever-changing dream.

"Put my baby down."

"Stop that, Chrysie. You're becoming irrational, and I can't have that. It upsets me."

Chrysie tried to move her hands again. She couldn't. They were bound behind her back, and she was lying on the back seat of a moving car.

She had to think. But her head was so foggy. Luisa must have drugged her. But how?

The coffee.

She swallowed past a tongue that seemed a foot thick. "Stop this car and untie me at once, Luisa."

"You know I can't do that."

Her feet were tied, as well. Still, she might be able to get them up high enough to kick Luisa in the back of the head. She tried, but her body simply wouldn't follow her commands. The drugs had turned her muscles to lead.

This was crazy. Luisa was a respected attorney. She didn't drug and kidnap people in broad daylight—only she had.

"Why are you doing this, Luisa?"

"You left me no choice."

"I didn't kill Jonathan."

"Of course you didn't, Cassandra. You were not even smart enough to divorce him. But someone had to get rid of him. He was running my clients off much faster than I could get new ones. And he insisted on a payback from my adoption service."

Adoption service. She didn't have an adoption service. She represented clients with legal problems. A payback. Blackmail. Oh, no. This was too bizarre. Luisa surely couldn't mean…

"I didn't know you had an adoption service."

"No, Josh would not have shared that with you. It would have put him in a bad light."

This was sick, so very sick. "Where did you get the babies, Luisa?"

"I did the public a service. Taking babies from people who can't even afford the children they already have and putting the innocent infants in the hands of people who can take care of them properly is a noble act."

Chrysie was stunned. With her psychological training, she should have recognized antisocial traits in Luisa long ago. There must have been signs. Jonathan must have guessed she was sick. But then, he'd been too busy cashing in on her depravities. Chrysie had never known her husband at all.

Chrysie lay quietly, trying to get her mind clear enough so she could find a way out of this. She didn't know what Luisa had planned for her, but she knew it would end in death. Luisa's strength lay in the very trait that may have led to her madness: she planned every detail to perfection.

"You're making a mistake, Luisa. You can't get away with this. People will find out that you're evil, and you'll lose your business. You'll go to jail."

"You are the one who's evil, Cassandra. Ask my stepsister's partner. Juan Hernandez will remind you how you killed his daughter. He tells everyone how he found Maria dead after she'd talked with you."

Chrysie groaned. Maria Hernandez. Detective Hernandez. She'd never connected the two. But then, she'd never seen him in the role of Maria's father.

That explained his attitude problems when he'd questioned her about Jonathan's death.

Chrysie's mind traveled back seven years. She'd just graduated and gone to work at a mental-health clinic near the museum district. Maria had been only sixteen. Her father had moved out. Her mother cried all the time. Her boyfriend had found someone else.

Suicidal. The word had been all but emblazoned on her forehead. Chrysie had warned her mother, insisted she have her daughter hospitalized. She'd promised to do that.

She hadn't. Instead she'd shared her prescriptions, handed over a full bottle of tranquilizers. And pretty, sweet, depressed Maria took all the pills at once.

Chrysie was drifting again. She had to fight the drugs, had to keep her thoughts on track. She couldn't die. The girls needed her. She just needed a better handle on Luisa's mental state, a better feel for just how delusional she'd become.

"Where are we going, Luisa?"

"To visit some acquaintances of mine."

Paid killers, no doubt. As Buckley and Rogers had been. Luisa must have had them killed, too, eliminated them because they hadn't killed Chrysie. Fear overrode the drugs, swelled like smoke and filled her burning lungs.

Chrysie had to work fast. Once Luisa turned her over to an assassin, it would be a hundred times harder to escape. She needed to keep Luisa talking until she decided the best way to get through to her.

"I met two of your friends, Luisa. Mac Buckley and Sean Rogers. Were they nice men?"

"They were thugs, actually. Very unlike the acquaintances you'll meet today. Do you like dogs?"

"I do. I love dogs."

"These are Dobermans."

"My roommate in college had a Doberman. He looked mean, but he was very sweet-tempered."

"These aren't, but they're very dependable. Sharp teeth. Trained to kill. And they have no fear or scruples. Just animal instincts. Killers should be like that, don't you think? We're almost there. If you listen, you can hear them barking."

Chrysie tried to steel herself against the terror. If she let it take over, she'd never get out of this alive.

You have to crawl inside their delusional world with them in order to reach them.

It must have been her Abnormal Psych professor who'd said that, though Chrysie doubted if Dr. Lucas had ever seen a patient like Luisa.

The car stopped and the driver's-side door flew open. Chrysie heard the dogs, barking and growling, rattling the fence. She imagined them on top of her, their teeth biting into her and ripping her flesh from her bones.

"Ride's over, Cassandra."

She didn't have to crawl into Luisa's world of madness. She was there.

JOSH DROVE LIKE a madman, flying from one lane to another, cutting people off and cursing the idiots who drove just like him and had the nerve to get in his way. There was only thing working in his favor—a very inconspicuous GPS surveillance tracking device that Grecco had installed on Luisa's car that very morning.

"Vehicle's stopped." Static followed Grecco's voice.

Damn! This was no time to lose his phone connection with Grecco. Josh turned up the volume on the speaker as he sped past an eighteen-wheeler.

"Location?"

"The road's not marked. She may be on private property."

Josh gave him a freeway exit number. "How do I stand?"

"You're a good ten miles away."

Josh switched to the far left lane, then got stuck between a couple of cars doing the speed limit while everyone else was over it by at least ten miles an hour.

"Nothing's marked in the area where she stopped, Josh. She may be in the middle of a pasture somewhere. I've alerted the cops. There are two squad cars trying to pick up her tail. You'll probably beat them up there."

He swerved around a white panel truck.

"Good luck, Josh."

"Yeah, luck." All his promises to keep Chrysie safe came down to luck. He should have leveled with her this morning, told her that he and Grecco suspected Luisa might have been the one Jonathan was blackmailing, the one who'd had him killed.

But it had never crossed his mind that Chrysie would hook up with anyone in Houston before he had had some kind of agreement with the police. She wouldn't have if she hadn't heard that her monsters were dead. She wouldn't have walked into danger if she hadn't felt so safe.

His exit was coming up, and traffic was backed up the length of the ramp. He hit the shoulder, not even slowing down as he squeezed through spots with no more than inches to spare. Cars honked. Drivers gave him the finger.

Two minutes later he spied the only fork in the road in sight, a dirt path that was little more than a cow trail meandering off through an open field. There was no sign that a car had been down it, but ten minutes was long enough for the dust to settle. Ten minutes was long enough for most anything.

God, don't let me be too late.

LUISA GRABBED Chrysie's hair and started yanking her from the car. Chrysie tried to fight, but with her hands and feet tied and her coordination diminished, she was almost helpless against the determinedly deranged woman. Rocks dug into Chrysie's back as she was dragged away from the car and to within inches of the tall chain-link fence.

The dogs' breath was hot on her flesh as the fierce animals threw themselves against the metal mesh, fighting to get to her. She wouldn't live five seconds inside that fence.

Chrysie's heart pounded, the fear so palpable it seeped from every pore of her body. She couldn't die. She couldn't. The girls needed her and she loved them so very, very much.

And there was Josh. She loved the way he smiled and teased. Loved his strength and even the way he spoiled his boys. Loved riding next to him over hills of snow in his beautiful sleigh.

Loved that he'd tried so hard to protect her.

Tears filled her eyes as she watched Luisa tie the end of a long rope to the gate, then carry the other end back to the car. Her plan was clear, well thought out, like all of her sick murders. She'd hold on to the rope as she started the car and jerked forward. Once the gate was open, she'd drop the rope and simply drive away.

Chrysie could all but feel the Dobermans' teeth tearing at her flesh. But Luisa wouldn't be around to see her suffering, no more than she'd seen Jonathan's death or any of the other deaths she'd ordered.

That was it, her altered state of reality. She was never in the wrong. Stealing babies was her way of helping them. Jonathan's weaknesses were the reason he couldn't be allowed to live. And if Chrysie had divorced Jonathan, she wouldn't have become involved it the plot to get rid of him.

And Luisa didn't kill. Paid thugs killed. Dogs killed. But never Luisa.

Crawl inside their delusional world....

Luisa rounded her car, rope in hand.

Chrysie started rolling, barely propelling herself in front of the car's tire before Luisa could pull away. For a minute she thought she'd read it wrong, believed that Luisa might just drive away and crush her beneath the wheels.

But the minute stretched to two or three. She was certain Luisa was thinking of a way around this. Her plan had been perfect, but Chrysie had spoiled it. The car door opened and then slammed shut. Chrysie watched Luisa stamp to the front of the car.

Before Luisa reached her, Chrysie caught a glimpse of dust flying in the distance like a whirlwind. Someone was coming and driving very fast. Possibly the owner of the dogs.

Or Josh.

It had to be Josh.

"What do you think you're doing, Chrysie?" Luisa's voice cracked with rage.

"If you want me dead, Luisa, you'll have to kill me. Not the dogs but you. Run over me. Shoot me. Strangle me. But you have to do it."

Luisa stared at her until her eyes glazed in fury before she grabbed Chrysie by her hair and dragged her away from the tire.

Chrysie rolled back before Luisa rounded the car. The feeling was coming back into her legs, and her coordination was drastically improving.

"Very well, Chrysie. We'll do this your way."

Luisa stamped away only to return a few seconds later holding a silver pistol and pointing it at Chrysie's right knee. Sweat poured from Luisa's forehead and dripped down her neck. Her hands shook. So did the gun.

This was not the way Luisa had planned this, but still she would win. She'd shatter Chrysie's kneecaps, and then when she pulled her away from the wheel, she wouldn't be able to roll back. The dogs would finish her off in seconds, just in time for Josh to find her bloodied mass of flesh.

Chrysie could not let that happen. She'd stayed alive against all odds for three years. She wouldn't die now.

Straining and calling on every ounce of strength she could muster, she swung her legs, slamming her taped ankles into Luisa's legs. Luisa teetered and fell, crashing to the hard ground beside Chrysie.

Luisa struggled to get up, but Chrysie raised her

upper body enough to slam her head into Luisa's, hitting so hard that her brain seemed to rattle against her skull.

When her head cleared, Josh was standing over them with his size-twelve foot planted firmly on Luisa's chest and a gun pointed at her head.

Concern clouded his dark eyes when he turned to Chrysie. "Are you all right?"

"I am now."

"You can't do this," Luisa said. "I have rights."

"Yes, you do," Josh agreed. "You have the right to do as I say or to become the next meal for six hungry dogs."

Josh grabbed his jacket from the hook by the back door. "Ok, boys. Time to pile in the car if we're going to make it to the airport on time."

"Wait," Danny called. "I have to get the present I made Jenny."

"It's still two days until Christmas," Josh reminded him.

"I know, but I want to give it to her now."

"It's just an old box with macaroni glued on it," Davy said.

"You're just saying that 'cause all the macaroni fell off yours."

"Can I take Mandy a cookie?" Davy said. "And take Chrysie one, too, so they can have a present?"

"Sure thing, buddy. Then we gotta rock and roll."

"I don't want to be a rock," Davy said.

"I can't find my reindeer horns," Danny yelled from somewhere down the hall.

"I've already got the costumes in the car. We're all set."

"Why aren't Chrysie and Mandy and Jenny spending the night with us like they used to?" Davy asked.

That was a very good question, and one that Josh couldn't answer. He'd stayed in Houston for three days after he'd almost lost Chrysie to the pack of wild dogs and the mad female attorney. She had come through the trauma like a trouper, which hadn't surprised him a bit.

The police had cleared up lots of details before he'd left, like arresting the owner of the dogs. The scumbag trained them to kill and then sold them to druggies to use against border patrol agents. Leave it to Luisa to know riffraff like that.

Luisa was undergoing a mental evaluation and awaiting trial for numerous crimes, though she'd never admitted to doing anything wrong. She'd specifically denied setting Chrysie up to take the rap for Jonathan's murder, but the evidence against her was pretty overwhelming. The only flaw had been Chrysie's leaving to go to the motel that night. But then she'd returned in time for Buckley and Rogers to salvage the original plan.

All charges had been dropped against Chrysie.

That's how Josh had left things.

It had been great to get back to Montana. If he never went to Houston again, it would be too soon. There were plenty of people who loved it, but there was way too much traffic in that city for him and not nearly enough fresh air.

But it wasn't until he'd returned to Montana that he'd realized how little he and Chrysie had talked about the future. He'd just expected she'd fly back up here and they'd take up where they'd left off. Why mess with a good thing?

It had taken a couple of short talks with Logan and one very long chat with Rachel for him to accept that women didn't think like that.

"I bet Chrysie likes our new car," Danny said as he and Davy crawled into the third-row seats of their new SUV.

"Let's hope so," Josh agreed. The car had been Rachel's suggestion. A man looking to acquire a large family needed a vehicle big enough for them to all fit. Apparently it was the same with a house.

Rachel was certain that Chrysie would have already considered and rejected the idea of moving into his one-bathroom and very crowded rustic cabin. He'd always planned to build a bigger place one day. Now he expected to start construction in the spring.

Josh shoved his hand into his pocket for the car

keys. His fingertips brushed the ring box. That was the one thing that made him a little nervous.

The engagement ring had been Logan's suggestion. Unfortunately his guidance didn't go beyond that, so the proposal was strictly up to Josh. He had no idea what he'd say, but he figured it would come to him when the time was right.

And that might just be tonight, after the Christmas pageant, when he took Chrysie and the girls back to the cabin on the Millers' ranch. They were staying through Christmas. He and the boys were excited about that. He'd even found the perfect present for Mandy: a cuddly black Lab.

Now all that was left was asking Chrysie to marry him and slipping that diamond ring on her finger.

HUMPHRIES BAR AND GRILL was more crowded and far noisier than Chrysie had ever seen it. Apparently half the town showed up for the annual community Christmas pageant, and half of them must have eaten at Humphries beforehand.

A quieter atmosphere would have suited her better. She had so much she wanted to talk about with Josh.

"I can push together two small tables, and the six of you can squeeze around that," the waitress said. "If you want a table for six, the wait will be about an hour."

"We'll squeeze," Josh said.

And squeeze they did. They were a mass of bumping elbows and hands and short, swinging legs. Chrysie didn't mind. She'd missed Josh terribly and missed the boys and even their chaos a lot more than she would have ever imagined.

But she was still nervous about being here. She'd gotten the feeling over the last few days that Josh was ready to rush into something permanent, and she needed time.

Besides, she'd married Jonathan impetuously. This time she wanted to take things more slowly, make certain she and Josh really knew each other, make certain the merged family situation could work. It was the psychologically sound thing to do.

"Boy, you should have seen us out snowmobiling yesterday," Danny said. "We were going over the hills like *pow, pow, pow.*" He slapped his hand against the table with every *pow* to demonstrate how they'd gone airborne with each crest.

"We don't have snow in Houston," Jenny said.

"Ever?"

"I don't think so. Do we, Mommy?"

"It snows occasionally but usually only a few flurries, nothing like it snows in Montana."

"Yeah, Montana's better," Davy said. "I asked for a sled for Christmas."

"Can I ride it?" Mandy asked.

"Well, it's going to be fast one, and you're just a little kid, so you might get hurt."

The waitress took their order and brought their drinks. Davy bumped Mandy's soda with his elbow, and the paper cup went sliding across the table.

Mandy wailed because her drink was spilled.

Davy howled because his pants got soaked and the kids in the pageant would say he went to the bathroom on himself.

Danny jumped out of his chair and ran to tell the waitress they had a spill. She followed him back with more paper napkins.

"Can we have a quarter to play a video game?" Davy asked. "They got a bunch of them in that other room."

Josh grinned. "That's the best idea you've had all night." He reached into his pocket and pulled out a handful of quarters. Eight eager hands opened like the mouths of hungry baby birds. He passed the coins out evenly and they were off and running.

Once they left, Josh reached for Chrysie's hands across the table. "Nice to have you home."

Here's where she had to be careful. It was difficult to think clearly when he touched her, impossible when he kissed her, the way he had at the airport.

"It's nice to see you and the boys," she said. "I've missed you."

"We've for sure missed you."

"No pancakes?" she teased, trying to keep the moment light.

"No good-night kisses."

"You can always visit me," she said.

His eyebrows arched. "Visit you in Houston?"

"That's where I live."

"I see." The teasing had disappeared from his voice.

She took a deep breath and plunged ahead before she weakened even more. "I've been offered a position as supervising staff psychologist at the clinic where I worked part-time before."

"What did you tell them?"

"I accepted the offer."

Josh let go of her hands. "I don't suppose anything I say would change that."

She took a deep breath. "I need to do this, Josh. I've been on the run for three years. I need time to find out what normalcy is before I make new commitments."

He looked away. "Not a lot of normalcy in the McCain clan. A small-town sheriff-rancher, a couple of rambunctious boys."

"This is as much for you as for me, Josh. We barely know each other, and most of the time we were together we were in a life-and-death struggle. We might feel differently about each other on a normal day-to-day basis."

"*You* might feel different. What you see is what you get with me, no matter what the situation."

She'd hurt him, and that was the last thing she'd wanted to do. But she was hurting, too. "I'm not suggesting we stop seeing each other, Josh. All I'm asking is for a little time."

"Time that you'll be in Houston, building a life there. Houston's not me, Chrysie. It's never going to be."

"Please, Josh. Don't just throw us away. Even if this doesn't work, we can at least be friends."

He shook his head and finally locked his gaze with hers. "I love you, Chrysie—or Cassandra, or whoever the hell you decide to be. I love you and I'd do anything for you—except be friends." He took the keys from his pocket and tossed them onto the table. "You take the car tonight and you can just drop it off at the airport whenever you leave."

"How will you get to the pageant? How will you get home?"

"Don't worry about us. The boys and I will catch a ride with somebody." He touched a hand to her shoulder. "Merry Christmas, Chrysie. I hope you have a hell of a life."

Her heart had never felt as empty as it did now, watching him walk out of her life without one backward glance.

CHRYSIE FOUGHT TEARS for the rest of the evening, especially during the pageant. This wasn't what she'd wanted. Josh was being unreasonable.

She shifted in her back-row seat as the pageant

came to a close. The girls had been perfect angels, thanks to Mrs. Larkey's letting them just dance around the tree during the four choruses of "We Wish You a Merry Christmas."

Chrysie gathered the girls' coats and hats as the performers prepared for the finale of bowing at center stage and parading down the center aisle and out the back door.

The reindeer led the parade. They were supposed to prance, but Danny was the lead reindeer, and he extended his arms like an airplane and flew down the aisle.

He stopped and waved when he saw her. She waved back. Davy didn't just wave, he stopped and gave her a big hug. "This is my friend," he announced to everybody in general.

The tears that had been burning at the back of her eyelids escaped and started to flow down her cheeks. The girls were still onstage waiting to take their bows when Chrysie saw Josh slip out the side door of the auditorium.

This might be the last time she ever saw him, and she couldn't let it end like this. She had to at least thank him for saving her life. She followed the last drummer boy out the back door and ran to catch up with Josh.

"Josh, wait!"

He didn't. She sloshed a few more feet, but she was losing ground.

"Josh? Wait!" she called even louder than before. If he heard, he was too stubborn to turn around. Well, she was stubborn, too. Stooping, she scooped up a handful of wet snow.

"Joooosh!" This time she yelled as loudly as she could.

He turned around just as she let the snowball fly. It hit him squarely between the eyes, and snow splattered all over his face. He strode toward her, looking livid. She might have just made a big mistake.

She turned and ran. She'd almost made it back to the door of the civic center when the return fire hit her in the back of the head.

This was war. She made another snowball, but before she could hurl it at Josh, she was hit from the right side. And the left. And in the stomach.

And then Danny jumped on her back and pushed a handful of snow down her collar. She lost her balance and fell to the snow with Danny still hanging on. Jenny and Davy piled on next. Mandy was the last.

They were all five laughing and hugging and rolling in the snow when Josh reached them, his face still stern. "That's enough, boys," he ordered. "Stand up right now and leave Chrysie alone. She doesn't want to play in the snow."

Oh, but she did. Why wouldn't she? Some people might need months to know that they were happier than they'd ever been in their lives. Some might never realize that they were in the perfect place for them. A few were crazy enough to find love and then let it slip away.

Josh extended his hand to help her up. She took it and pulled him into the pile with them. "Marry me, Josh," she whispered. "Marry me, for Christmas."

"Why?"

"Because I love you and everything about you, especially your rambunctious sons. Because I want to keep loving you for the rest of my life."

"What about Houston?"

"I could never live there," she teased. "No snowball fights."

And there in the middle of a tumbling mass of laughing, hugging kids—their kids—and the cheers of half the population of Aohkii, Josh kissed her.

She kissed him back, and this time tears of happiness ran down her cheeks. She was home to stay.

* * * * *

New York Times *bestselling author
Linda Lael Miller is back with a new romance
featuring the heartwarming McKettrick family
from Silhouette Special Edition.*

*SIERRA'S HOMECOMING
by Linda Lael Miller*

*On sale December 2006,
wherever books are sold.*

Turn the page for a sneak preview!

Soft, smoky music poured into the room.

The next thing she knew, Sierra was in Travis's arms, close against that chest she'd admired earlier, and they were slow dancing.

Why didn't she pull away?

"Relax," he said. His breath was warm in her hair.

She giggled, more nervous than amused. What was the matter with her? She was attracted to Travis, had been from the first, and he was clearly attracted to her. They were both adults. Why not enjoy a little slow dancing in a ranch-house kitchen?

Because slow dancing led to other things. She took

a step back and felt the counter flush against her lower back. Travis naturally came with her, since they were holding hands and he had one arm around her waist.

Simple physics.

Then he kissed her.

Physics again—this time, not so simple.

"Yikes," she said, when their mouths parted.

He grinned. "Nobody's ever said that after I kissed them."

She felt the heat and substance of his body pressed against hers. "It's going to happen, isn't it?" she heard herself whisper.

"Yep," Travis answered.

"But not tonight," Sierra said on a sigh.

"Probably not," Travis agreed.

"When, then?"

He chuckled, gave her a slow, nibbling kiss. "Tomorrow morning," he said. "After you drop Liam off at school."

"Isn't that…a little…soon?"

"Not soon enough," Travis answered, his voice husky. "Not nearly soon enough."

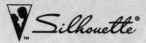

HARLEQUIN *Romance*®

**From the Heart.
For the Heart.**

Get swept away into the Outback
with two of Harlequin Romance's
top authors.

Coming in December...

Claiming the
Cattleman's Heart
BY BARBARA HANNAY

And in January don't miss...

Outback Man Seeks Wife
BY MARGARET WAY

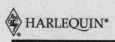

HARLEQUIN®

American | ROMANCE®

IS PROUD TO PRESENT

COWBOY VET
by Pamela Britton

Jessie Monroe is the last person on earth
Rand Sheppard wants to rely on, but he needs
a veterinary technician—yesterday—and she's the
only one for hire. It turns out the woman who
destroyed his cousin's life isn't who Rand thought
she was. And now she's all he can think about!

"Pamela Britton writes the kind of
wonderfully romantic, sexy, witty romance
that readers dream of discovering
when they go into a bookstore."

—*New York Times* bestselling author
Jayne Ann Krentz

**Cowboy Vet *is available from
Harlequin American Romance in December 2006.***

www.eHarlequin.com   HARPBDEC

REQUEST YOUR FREE BOOKS!

2 FREE NOVELS PLUS 2 FREE GIFTS!

HARLEQUIN®

INTRIGUE®

Breathtaking Romantic Suspense

YES! Please send me 2 FREE Harlequin Intrigue® novels and my 2 FREE gifts. After receiving them, if I don't wish to receive any more books, I can return the shipping statement marked "cancel." If I don't cancel, I will receive 6 brand-new novels every month and be billed just $4.24 per book in the U.S., or $4.99 per book in Canada, plus 25¢ shipping and handling per book and applicable taxes, if any*. That's a savings of close to 15% off the cover price! I understand that accepting the 2 free books and gifts places me under no obligation to buy anything. I can always return a shipment and cancel at any time. Even if I never buy another book from Harlequin, the two free books and gifts are mine to keep forever.

182 HDN EEZ7   382 HDN EEZK

Name _____ (PLEASE PRINT) _____

Address _____ Apt. _____

City _____ State/Prov. _____ Zip/Postal Code _____

Signature (if under 18, a parent or guardian must sign)

Mail to Harlequin Reader Service®:

IN U.S.A.
P.O. Box 1867
Buffalo, NY
14240-1867

IN CANADA
P.O. Box 609
Fort Erie, Ontario
L2A 5X3

Not valid to current Harlequin Intrigue subscribers.

Want to try two free books from another line?
Call 1-800-873-8635 or visit www.morefreebooks.com.

* Terms and prices subject to change without notice. NY residents add applicable sales tax. Canadian residents will be charged applicable provincial taxes and GST. This offer is limited to one order per household. All orders subject to approval. Credit or debit balances in a customer's account(s) may be offset by any other outstanding balance owed by or to the customer. Please allow 4 to 6 weeks for delivery.

HI06

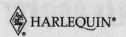

HARLEQUIN®

INTRIGUE®

COMING NEXT MONTH

#957 FORCE OF THE FALCON by Rita Herron
Eclipse
After a string of bizarre animal attacks near Falcon Ridge,
Brack Falcon finds a woman left for dead. But protecting
Sonya Silverstein means opening his long-dormant heart.

#958 TRIGGERED RESPONSE by Patricia Rosemoor
Security Breach
Brayden Sloane is a wanted man. He remembers an accident, an
explosion. Was he responsible? Only Claire Fanshaw knows for sure,
but how will she react to his touch?

#959 RELUCTANT WITNESS by Kathleen Long
Fate brings Kerri Nelson and Wade Sorenson back together to save
the life of her son, the only witness to a heinous crime.

#960 PULL OF THE MOON by Sylvie Kurtz
He's a Mystery
She's at Moongate Mansion for a story. He thinks she's an impostor.
But before history repeats Valerie Zea and Nicholas Galloway will
have to put their doubts aside to solve the mystery behind an
heiress's kidnapping.

#961 LAKOTA BABY by Elle James
Returning soldier Joe Lonewolf must enter the ugly underbelly of his
tribe if he's to rescue the baby boy he's never seen.

#962 UNDERCOVER SHEIK by Dana Marton
When Dr. Sadie Kauffman is kidnapped by desert bandits in Beharrain,
her only salvation lies in Sheik Nasir, the king's brother, who's trying
to stop a tyrant from plunging the country into civil war.

www.eHarlequin.com